# KEITH BURKE

# The Last Goodbye

Copyright © 2020 by Keith Burke

All rights reserved. No part of this publication may be reproduced, stored or transmitted in any form or by any means, electronic, mechanical, photocopying, recording, scanning, or otherwise without written permission from the publisher. It is illegal to copy this book, post it to a website, or distribute it by any other means without permission.

First edition

This book was professionally typeset on Reedsy.
Find out more at reedsy.com

*To Sam, for being my lighthouse in the storm.*

# 1

## JACK

My name is Jack Richardson. I'm just like you. I was born in a town just like yours. I grew up on a street just like the one you grew up on. But that, I'm afraid, is where the similarities end. My life and my story ended up being beyond anything I could have imagined. And like so many stories through the ages, mine starts with a girl.

I met Jess Miller when I was 17 years old, and I know it sounds cliché but the moment I laid eyes on her I knew my life would never be the same. Do you believe in love at first sight? No? Well neither did I until I saw her. I know what you are thinking, it's just first love, it happens to all of us, but this was more than that. I felt it in my bones. I felt it in the deepest recesses of my being. I felt like a magnet being drawn towards her. And I knew that no matter how I tried to fight it I would be pulled into her orbit. So, I didn't try to fight it.

It was a typical Tuesday morning, nothing special or interesting about the day. I woke up, drank my body weight in coffee, grabbed a wrinkled shirt from the pile of clothes on the floor and ran out the door just in time to

catch the bus. I had first period math with Mrs. Andrews, a decrepit old woman who I'm pretty sure was around when the abacus was invented. Her gray hair was pulled up in a messy bun and her sweater was pretty much made up entirely of cat hair.

I had stalled as much as I could, so I closed my locker to head to class and that is when I saw her. As sappy as it sounds, time stopped. I can remember that moment like it was yesterday, floating above myself like I was having one of those out-of-body-experiences, as if I were watching myself watch her. People say there are a few moments that define your life. Without a doubt, this was

defining moment of mine. She was perfection.

Jess wasn't the type of girl I usually went for; not that I really ever went for too many girls, to be honest. I was always a bit of a loner. She had on raggedy combat boots that were half laced so the leftovers dragged alongside her just waiting to trip her. She wore head-to-toe black. She was your quintessential Goth girl, putting on an edgy front to hide her soft, chewy, emotional center. To me she was radiant, and no amount of black eyeliner could hide that.

I couldn't have had less in common with her. My dad had been a star athlete growing up and always pushed me to follow in his footsteps. My mom, on the other hand, wanted me to go to an Ivy League school. So, in her mind, studying was always the priority. I was a disappointment to both of them. I was a jock, and not a particularly good one at that. But when you are blessed with my academic abilities or lack thereof, sports are often the only way to try and make a future for yourself. I was a solid second-string quarterback on the football team. Sounds impressive, right? Well, that is until I tell you that we had not won a single game the entire season, or the last two seasons. So, like I said, not all that impressive.

But I digress. I fell in love with Jess from the very first second I saw her. I actually felt my heart skip a beat. We didn't end up meeting for a few weeks because I was too scared to approach her. Every day I would be giddy with excitement for the chance to just see her, even if it was for only a few seconds. I would daydream about her, and at night I would dream about what it would be like to actually have the courage to say hi to her. This went on for weeks, until fate, or whatever it is you believe in, intervened and we ran into each other...literally.

I was in town running some errands for my parents. I came out of the shop and pretty much knocked her over.

Paying attention was never one of my virtues. I didn't even realize it was her until she hit the ground.

I felt horrible. Why did the Universe hate me so much!

I had played out our first meeting so many times in my head. I would be charming and suave, and she would fall for me on the spot. But dreams and reality rarely collide. The reality of what happened was basically the opposite of romantic fireworks. Instead of being debonair, I helped her up and just walked away awkwardly without saying a word. I beat myself up all night. I finally had the chance with the girl of my dreams and I completely blew it. Spectacularly blew it! All I could hope was maybe she would think I was a mute or something. That was the best-case scenario. Why couldn't I have just said something? Anything? "I'm sorry," "hello," either of those would have been fine.

The next day at school I replayed the encounter on a loop in my head. I was lost in my thoughts when I heard a voice from behind me. "You owe me a coffee." I turned around and it was her. I just stared. I could feel my face turning red. The seconds that passed felt like hours. Say something! Anything!

I finally managed to spit out one word. "Hi." She waited for what also felt like an eternity and then the corner of her mouth turned slightly upwards into a smirk. She said hi back and my heart melted. One word was all it took. I was a puddle on the floor. The rest is history, as they say.

From that day on we were inseparable. It was like we had been searching for each other our entire lives. And we had, but more on that later. We finished high school that year and Jess was accepted to film school at NYU. There was never even a question as to what I was going to do, I packed up what little I had and said bye to my parents and followed her to New York. And that is when our lives really began.

It didn't take her long to ditch the Goth look in favor of something more natural. I joked with her that she ditched her "signature" look because she fell so in love with me that all the world became brighter. But that only made her roll her eyes. The truth is once we got to New York she didn't need to make a statement with her appearance, she could accomplish much more with her films. Underneath all the black hair dye and mascara, Jess's

natural hair color was a light brown and her hazel eyes sparkled against her alabaster skin.

That first year in New York was magic. We moved into our first apartment together. It was such a dump, there were rats and roaches that were bigger than Jess. The hot water worked maybe once a week and the electricity was just as sporadic. We spent many a night hanging out by candlelight. But it was dump and it was perfect. We were so in love with the city, so in love with each other. It was like the party you never wanted to leave.

Every day was a new adventure whether it was her following me to check out some new indie band I'd heard of— a band that 9 times out of 10 was terrible, but she would always be there right next to me with a smile—or it was the two of us having a picnic in Central Park, Jess falling asleep on my legs. Those were my favorite days, just watching her sleep while the world moved at warp speed around us. I should have told her more often that those were my favorite days. I should have done a lot of things differently, but you can't change things, no matter how much you want to.

It wasn't always sunshine and rainbows, there were hard times too. When we were twenty, we found out that Jess was pregnant. It was unexpected and neither of us was ready to be parents. But the more we thought about it the more excited we became. Every time I thought about Jess waddling around the apartment pregnant and miserable, it just made me smile. I knew I always wanted children it was just sooner than I had planned. We didn't have much, but we had love. The rest we could and would figure out together.

It turned out the Universe agreed with our initial apprehension because Jess lost the baby shortly into her second trimester. It nearly broke her but together we figured out how to move on and let it go. Well, you never really let something like that go, I don't know, you just learn how to deal with the pain. I think neither of us would have been able to make it if we didn't have each other. That is how you know it's real. When the awful parts of life happen, you cling to each other like never before. And I knew that I never wanted to experience one day without her by my side.

I proposed to her six months ago with a ring my dad helped me buy because I barely made enough to pay the rent. If I'm being honest, I still had no idea what I wanted to do with my life. I joked that I was still a work in progress. I was the polar opposite of Jess. She had known her entire life that she wanted to be a documentary filmmaker. I envied that about her. She always knew who she was and where she was going. Everything about her just wanted me to be a better man. I thought about doing some elaborate proposal like one of those you see on YouTube or something but then I realized that just wasn't us, so I did it on a normal weekend without any pomp and circumstance.

She was wearing an old pair of my boxer shorts and one of my tank tops. Her hair went in 500 different directions as it always did when she first woke up and she had a little sleep crust in the corner of her eyes. She was never more beautiful than in that moment. We both had a love for Oscar Wilde so when I proposed I recited one of our favorite quotes. "To live is the rarest thing in the world, most people exist, that is all." She replied with the rest of the quote, "And what is rarer still is to love without boundaries." It just made sense for us because I wasn't interested in anything other than a life with Jess. And when I popped the question, I'd never seen a bigger smile on her face in the entire five years that we were together. She leaned in so she was looking right into my eyes and just whispered, "Yes."

What Jess and I had was everything, the kind of love you only see in the movies in some ridiculous montage.

Which is just not real life, but it was for us. Our friends said we were two halves of the same soul. Kindred spirits, yin and yang, you get the idea. If they only knew how right they were.

By now I'm sure you've noticed that I keep talking about Jess and me in the past. Well there is a good reason for that.

I'm dead.

## 2

## JESS

In my life, four moments have changed me forever.

Three of those were with Jack. The second was the day I saw him in school, so many years ago. The first, well that was a long time before he even knows about. He loves to tell the story of how he saw me at the end of the hallway at school and how that was the moment his life would never be the same. I loved hearing him talk about the Goth girl who spun the world he knew on its side. He was always so cute when he told the story of 'how we met' that I never had the heart to tell him it just wasn't true. Jack and I actually met when we were six years old, he just didn't know it.

I was trying to save money to buy a new doll I wanted.

My mom decided that age six would be the perfect time to teach me the value of a dollar. Mom was a forward thinker, maybe a little too forward sometimes. Children don't really care about stock portfolios and saving for retirement. But she would say that 'one can never be too prepared'. If I wanted to get the doll, I would have to pay for it myself. So, I decided to start a lemonade stand in front of our house to make money.

It was a hot summer day, a perfect day to make some money. That summer had been extra humid so I was selling lemonade faster than I could make it to the kids and parents in the neighborhood. I was in the middle of making up a new batch when Jason Hawkins came barreling over towards my little stand. He was the school and neighborhood bully. He was twice the size of most of us and he wasn't the brightest crayon in the box. He was big enough that whatever he wanted he got because all the rest of the kids— and some of the parents, probably—were afraid of him. The same went for his dad, Old Man Hawkins. My mom used to joke that they were actual Neanderthals who had managed to escape extinction. Jason lumbered up to my stand breathing heavily like he always did and demanded a cup of lemonade on the house. When I refused, he knocked my lemonade stand over and pushed me down. There was nothing I could do but sit there and cry. My parents were conveniently nowhere to be seen. After he left, that's when I first saw Jack. He didn't live in the neighborhood, so I'd never seen him before, he just happened to be riding around on his skateboard with his friends when Jason was ruining my day.

He came up on his skateboard and didn't say a word. At first, I thought he was just one of Jason's pack of goons.

I was waiting for him to stomp on what was left of my lemonade stand. But he didn't. He just took my hand and helped me up. He gave me a half smile; he had one of those slightly crooked yet totally adorable smirk kind of smiles. He wiped a tear from my cheek and just helped me pick everything up and set my stand up again. The whole time he never said a word. He smelled like bubble gum and the slightly acrid aroma of burnt rubber, no doubt from his wheels rolling on asphalt for hours. When everything was back where it should be, he just looked at me, and I looked back. We stared at each other for what felt like an eternity. There was a kindness in his eyes that made me feel safe, that made me feel like I was home. He made me feel all that without saying a word. That moment with Jack was the first that changed my life. Until then, and not surprisingly because I was only six, I had no idea what love even was. I thought my heart was going to beat out of my chest. In my short life, I had probably read a thousand stories about princesses finding their princes. They all seemed so fantastical but here he was, my very own Prince Charming who had saved me from the ogre that was Jason Hawkins. Before I could say anything, his friends called to him. He turned to me and reached into his pocket, pulled out a dollar, and put it in my tip jar. He smirked again and just said "bye", that's all, and hopped on his skateboard to catch up with his friends. I never even said a word to him. It's no wonder he doesn't remember. To this day I can picture the sun bouncing off his dark brown hair and the way his blue eyes shone like two tiny oceans. I remember being sad for weeks. I put up the lemonade stand every weekend for a year just hoping to see him again, but he never came back. My mom thought she had succeeded in making me understand the value of money. But I couldn't care less about money or the dozens of dolls I was able to buy. I only cared about the blue-eyed boy who had skated in and out of my life.

I thought about telling him the truth so many times, but it just seemed so trivial and I didn't want to ruin it for him. But now that is my biggest regret. He never knew the truth, never knew that I'd been in love with him for pretty much my entire life. As the years went by, he was always in my thoughts. The boy on the skateboard who changed everything. And though time had changed him, and he looked different, I knew in an instant that Jack was the boy from my lemonade stand, when we 'met' in high school.

It was his eyes. His features may have changed, his voice may have deepened, but his eyes hadn't. Like most of the boys in his class he was trying to seem like more of a man, so he had a decent amount of scruff on his face, more than most of the other boys. Time had changed me as well. After my dad passed I went through a pretty rough patch. I didn't see much of a point to most things, life included. I was the walking cliché that used black eyeliner, hair dye and clothes to hide my pain. But that all changed when Jack came back into my life. As soon as I saw his eyes I just knew it was him, the boy who turned my world upside down.

When I was little my mom used to tell me all these stories from when she was younger. Before she met my dad, she was a flight attendant and had traveled the world and seen amazing places and done amazing things. At the time, I thought those stories were all made up because, well, she was my boring mom, she couldn't possibly have had all those adventures. The one thing that has always stuck with me is how she said that life is just a series of moments. Some perfect, some interesting, some terrible and some that change your life forever.

The third moment that changed my life was when I lost him. We were supposed to have friends over for dinner, so I was going to make pasta. In the middle of cooking I

realized I forgot to grab tomatoes. Jack hated them but he would always just pick around them. Those are the little things I am going to miss. I'm never going to clean another dish that has a mushy pile of his uneaten tomatoes on it.

What if I had made chicken instead of pasta, would Jack still be here? I had made him go to the place where he died. It was my fault. He had wanted to go out to dinner, but I insisted on cooking. He is gone because of me. No one prepares you for that kind of guilt, the what-ifs of life. What if I we had lived somewhere else? What if we gone out to dinner? Would that have changed anything? Would I still be preparing to bury the one person I made sense with, the one person I never had to be anything other than myself with? How was that fair? I lost the love of my life because of one errand.

I had just put the pasta into the boiling water when I heard the first shot. It's New York City, so gunshots are not unheard of, but these were different. I felt the sound in my stomach, in my heart. I don't know how I knew I just did. It felt like a piece of me died in that moment. I knew right away something happened. I knew my world was once again flipped upside down. I ran out the door and down the stairs, leaving the linguini in the pot boiling away. By

the time I got back several hours later the water had evaporated and the pasta had turned to ash...just like my world. For a split second I thought about letting the place fill with smoke so I could be with Jack, but the police officer who walked me back to the apartment took care of it.

When I look back on that night it's pretty much a blur. I can remember turning the corner and running. I can remember there was so much blood. It sounds crazy but one of the things I distinctly remember seeing was a box of Lucky Charms cereal sprayed red. The poor leprechaun's face was nearly covered in blood. It's weird what you remember. I think it's just the mind's way of coping with trauma, but I can't picture Jack lying there...and thank God. I get to remember him the way I want to remember him, smiling that crooked little smile with his bright blue eyes looking right back at me.

The rest of that evening played out like a silent movie. I just sat there while the EMTs tried their best to revive Jack. The officers kept asking me questions, but I couldn't hear anything. Their mouths moved in slow motion, their lips distorted by the flashing red and blue lights. I was numb...empty...hollow. The reason I woke up in the morning,

the person I clung to when I went to bed at night, wasn't there anymore. My Jack was gone. I didn't know what to do with myself. Once we got back upstairs and the officer had taken the pot of ash off the stove, he tried asking me a few more questions. He asked me about my relationship with the "victim"; it was that word that snapped me out of my daze. I looked up at the officer. He was just a kid, like me. He didn't know how to handle the situation any more than I did. I said softly to him, "His name was Jack Richardson. He is...was...my fiancé." Hearing the word "was" come out of my mouth was enough for me to crack. I just sobbed and sobbed till I had no tears left. By that point Andrea from next door had come over to help, but what could she do. She was new to the building and we had just started to get to know each other. I had told Jack that I wanted to get to know her better. She tried her best to cheer me up but there was no way to make this better, no way to make it go away. In the end, she just held me and let me cry. I was grateful for her effort, but it did nothing to make this horrible day any better.

I'm sure you've heard stories about people who have had near-death experiences and how they say that your entire life flashes before your eyes when your time is up.

Something similar happens to people who have experienced sudden and profound tragedies. It's not so much that your life flashes before your eyes, more so that your mind brings the seemingly mundane to the forefront and puts a different spin on it. When Jack was alive he used to do this thing. He used to trace an infinity symbol on the inside of my palm. The first time he did it I asked him why and he said that he and I were forever, just like the symbol. There was no end and no beginning for us; we just were. He was always such a sap. I used to bust his balls about it, but I secretly loved how much of a hopeless romantic he could be. And now that was gone. My forever, my infinity was no more. I had started the day as half of a pair, partners, best friends, lovers, soon-to-be spouses.

Now I was just me. Just Jess. Jess the widow. Except, I wasn't even a widow because I never got to marry him. There isn't even a word for what I was now. I was just broken.

# 3

# JACK

Love is a fickle thing, as the saying goes. But true love...that's a whole different ballgame. I'm not talking about your run-of-the-mill infatuation. I'm talking about TRUE love, the kind of love that wakes you up in the middle of the night because you miss that person so much, even though they are right next to you. The kind of love that fills a hole in your heart that you didn't even know was there. The kind of love that makes you do incredibly stupid things. All judgment goes out the window the minute you find that person. That's what Jess and I had... until I died.

Jess had asked me to run downstairs to the bodega to pick up some tomatoes. We were having friends over and she was making pasta. Being the dutiful fiancé, I hustled down the street. But I have to be honest, we weren't the best at adulting, but we were faking our way through it. We were still getting used to the idea of being engaged. So, every now and then we would have a dinner party with another couple because it's what adults do, right? You make dinner and you drink wine instead of ordering pizza and drinking cheap beer from a can. Who knew my life would end

because of a trip to the bodega? And for tomatoes of all things; I hated tomatoes! As fate would have it, at exactly the same time I was grabbing tomatoes from the bin, a kid decided that he was going to rob this particular bodega.

Well, the short of it is—because, like I said, this story is about love, not death—there was an exchange of shots between the owner of the bodega and the kid, and I was caught in the crossfire. It's so depressing when you think about it, dying because of the one food in the world you can't stand. But that's what happened. Jess heard the shots from our apartment and came running, but by the time she got there I was almost gone.

Things get cloudy when you are dying, in case you want to prepare yourself for when it's your time. I remember looking up at her and she was screaming and crying, but I couldn't hear her. I wanted to tell her that I wasn't in pain. I wanted to tell her a thousand things, but then I was gone. And then I wasn't gone. My view had changed. I wasn't looking up at her any longer. I was watching her leaning over me. I had crossed over. I didn't float out of my body or anything like that. It happened more in the blink of an eye. One moment I was there, the next I wasn't.

She tried to revive me.

Surreal is watching your fiancée try to revive your dead body while you watch. The paramedics also tried but there was nothing they could do. That is not where this story ends; it's the beginning.

People talk all the time about how their boyfriend or their wife is their soulmate. For the most part, people who say that are wrong. Soulmates are rare. How do I know this, you ask? Well, just after I died, a Guardian Angel told me. It turns out I didn't have a Guardian Angel when I died because my other half, Jess, was still living. So, one was "assigned" to me to help me move on to the next plane, if that is what I chose to do. He was dressed in a strange- looking red coat and his name was Alistair. You'd think I'd be pissed; I was at the start of my life with Jess and in an instant, I was dead...at 22. But the funny thing is, I wasn't. The anger goes away when your life ends, love is all that remains; well, that and the ache, the ache to feel, the ache to live, the ache to have one more minute with the person who means the most in the world to you.

That never really goes away. So many people just go through the motions, they never really live. We take so much for granted in life, that there is always tomorrow. But what if there isn't? It's hard to put into words what the ache

feels like. It's not a physical pain because the physical you no longer exists. I guess you could say it is a spiritual pain, a longing.

Alistair told me Jess and I were genuine, honest-to- God soulmates. That we had lived many lives together and we were destined to find our way back to each other in each life. And because of that fact, I was given a choice. Head on "upstairs" and wait for Jess, or stay and be Jess's Guardian Angel until it's her time. I know we've just met, but I think you can figure out what my decision was. I decided to stay...for her. It is still a lot to process, even now, the whole idea of God, Angels, Guardian Angels. I always believed in God. But having faith in something and knowing for a fact all of it is real are two different things altogether.

On paper, being Jess's Guardian Angel sounded perfect.

I wouldn't have to leave her, and I could watch over her and keep her safe. The reality is something different. For starters, Jess will never be able to see me. It gets a bit technical, but humans don't possess the visual acuity to see the plane we exist on. Or at least that's what I was able to piece together from what Alistair told me. Second, not only is it impossible for me to interact with Jess, I'm

not able to affect anything in her world. There is no way to let her know that I'm here. As far as she knows, the moment I died in the bodega, I was gone for good. So, I had to sit there helplessly and watch the love of my life get crushed by my death. I now understood how Sisyphus feels.

No matter what I do, no matter how hard I try, I can't change or take away her pain. The first day, once the police left, she didn't get out of bed. She just kept smelling my pillow—which no doubt still smelled like me—and bursting into tears. There really is no other sound in the world more haunting than the wail that emanates from a person in a state of pure grief. That was when I felt the ache for the first time. It felt like an arrhythmia in my heart. But I didn't have a heart anymore. Where my heart used to be is where I felt the ache.

What good is being a Guardian Angel if I can't comfort Jess, hold her, stroke her hair, and let her know that everything will be all right? I just had to sit there and watch her despair unfold in slow motion. It was cruel. By the second day, she had managed to at least get out of bed to eat. But that was only because our neighbor Andrea forced her to. Death is a funny thing; you see what people are really made of. The people I thought would be there for

Jess weren't. Maybe it was too hard for them, too difficult for them to see Jess in pain, or maybe they weren't the people I thought they were. But this stranger was there for her.

The day after I died, the ache got worse. It felt as if my entire being was tethered to Jess like a rubber band, and our souls were trying to come back together, across time, across space, across death. But they couldn't reconnect. I didn't have a body anymore, but that didn't stop the ache. Nothing stops the ache, I came to find out.

The third day after I died was my funeral. Man, those things are depressing. Everyone sitting around in black, crying and cursing the universe because I was taken in my prime. I guess I should be flattered that so many people miss me. I felt like I was watching a movie, but it wasn't a movie. It was real, and I was—well, my body anyway— nestled peacefully in a coffin. The mortician had combed my hair differently and had gone a bit crazy with the blush on my cheeks. Plus, I was wearing a suit. I didn't even own a suit. I looked like a young version of my grandfather. I didn't look like me. But I guess it really didn't matter.

Jess and I had talked once about what we would want if we died. We both agreed we didn't want some somber affair. We wanted the other to celebrate our life. But that's easier said than done, as it turns out. Jess sat in the front row looking catatonic. The pastor, whom I'd never met before, prattled on about how I died so young, blah, blah, blah. I didn't even know this guy but here he was reading from his script where my name had been inserted. Then Jess came to the lectern to speak.

She wiped a tear and crumpled up her Kleenex. "I don't even know where to start. I can't believe he is gone," she said before getting choked up.

She continued, "Jack and I met when we were six. He thinks we met when we were seventeen, but the truth is he came to my rescue when he didn't know anything about me. That was just the kind of guy he was. I've loved him my entire life. He never knew I was the little girl with the lemonade stand he helped fix. I never told him and now I'll never be able to tell him."

Ache...

The memories came flooding back to me like a tidal wave. I had completely forgotten all about the girl and her lemonade stand. How could I have not known? All these years she just let me believe that we met in high school. That was the thing about Jess; even when you thought you knew everything about her, she could still surprise you. She continued, "Jack was my home. To quote our favorite author, Oscar Wilde, 'You don't love someone for their looks, or their clothes, or their fancy car, but because they sing a song that only you can hear.'" She choked out the last couple words before she started to crumble again. But my Jess is strong. She gathered herself and looked up in my direction; except she couldn't see me, she could only see everyone grieving. Then she turned and walked over to my casket and whispered, "Jack, I miss your song."

ACHE...

I wanted to run to her and hold her. I wanted to scream to her that I was there and everything was going to be fine. But I couldn't do anything except watch her shatter into a million pieces. She was a scattered puzzle that I couldn't put back together. After the funeral, everyone went back to our apartment. Jess's mom was there to make sure everything was taken care of. Jess and her mom haven't always seen eye to eye, but I could tell by the look on her face that Jess was grateful she was...well...being a mom, bossing everyone around, and making sure that no one was hassling her.

Jess's mom Erika and I didn't always get along either.

The thing with her is she always means well, so you can't really get too mad at her. So, while she orders everyone around and tries to make everything perfect, you usually just grumble to yourself that she's driving you crazy. She never thought I was the best fit for her only daughter.

Jess, of course, was brilliant and there was never any doubt that anything she wanted in her life would be hers. Erika thought I, on the other hand, was a bit of a slacker who, to quote her, "will never really live up to his potential." It's kinda funny; who knew how right she was. The one thing she never doubted though was how much I loved her daughter. When she'd had a bit too much wine, she used to just watch us and muse about how she wished Jess's father had looked at her the way I looked at Jess. It was the closest thing I ever got to a compliment from Erika Miller.

Jess was sitting in the corner staring at a picture of the two of us on the mantle when Erika took a break from barking at people to come and sit down beside her. Jess snapped out of her daze. "Hey, Mom." Erika brushed her hair around her ears. "How are you holding up?" Jess picked up the picture of us and hugged it before replying. "I don't know...numb...it doesn't feel real...I feel like he is still here, Mom. Is that crazy?" Erika smiled softly. "No, sweetheart, the good ones never really leave us, they always stay here," she said, patting her heart gently. Jess just listened, a single tear rolling down her cheek. "You didn't really like him, Mom." Erika stiffened up and adjusted her blouse and pearls. "Quite the contrary, my love, I was quite fond of Jack. No matter what was going on, I knew as long as you were with Jack you were safe and you were loved. That is all a mother can hope for. Not that I ever would've told him that. You have to keep men on their toes, otherwise they go all soft". Jess leaned her head on Erika's shoulder and started to cry. If I still had a heart, it would have broken in that moment, just watching her try to hold it together in front of everyone.

Ache...

That's the other funny thing about dying; you find out what people thought of you. Well, that is if you are lucky—or unlucky—enough to stick around. Who knew Erika actually liked me all these years. If I were a betting man, I would have said she'd be thanking her lucky stars that I kicked the bucket.

Eventually the reception ended, and Jess and her mom spent a good 30 minutes in the kitchen trying to figure out where to put all the casseroles people brought over. I still don't understand why people always bring casseroles to funerals. Maybe mix it up! Who doesn't love a good fruit salad? In case you haven't noticed, sarcasm is how I deal with everything. Not everything changes when you die.

The other tricky thing about being a Guardian Angel is time. Time doesn't mean the same thing it does to humans. I found that out the first time Alistair took me "upstairs"— and by "upstairs", I don't mean the 2nd floor of our apartment building; I'm talking about the pearly white gates, the Big H. Alistair's job was to show me the ropes, so to speak.

Jess had just turned in for the night. She put on a pair of my sweatpants and one of my t-shirts and curled up on my side of the bed. It made me smile because she used to make a fuss about how she could only sleep on one side of the bed, her side. I guess both sides of the bed were technically hers now. I was sitting in this ratty old club chair that I bought when Jess and I started dating. She used to joke that it went with nothing in the apartment and she was going to throw it away one of these days. I would

just smirk back and tell her the chair goes with me, and if it goes, I go. Reluctantly she agreed, but I knew she still hated it.

Things were silent in the apartment when Alistair appeared. He had this bad habit of just appearing out of nowhere and that's what he did that night. I was sitting in my chair, getting ready to watch Jess sleep for the third night in a row, when he materialized right in front of me. It's not really possible to scare a Guardian Angel, but man that guy loved to try and give you a heart attack.

I guess I didn't really explain the whole Guardian Angel thing very well. First off, we don't have wings. Guardian Angels were human once, so we pretty much just look human. Now Angel Angels, they were never human, so they look way more impressive with their big wings and all. I look how I looked the day I died; well, minus the blood and the giant hole in my chest. I died in a pair of jeans, a dark gray hoodie, and some black Chuck Taylors. I don't know if this is how I will look forever, but seeing how Alistair looked, I'm guessing that might be the case. At least I'm comfortable.

Alistair, I'm pretty sure, was a British soldier when he was alive. He still wore the standard uniform for the

British redcoat soldiers from the 18th and 19th centuries. So, since his outfit hadn't changed, I was pretty sure I'd be rocking the slacker hoodie look till the end of days.

Alistair adjusted his coat. "You're supposed to watch over her, not stare at her like some sort of stalker while she sleeps." He was right, but I'd been a Guardian Angel for three days and it's not like you get a handbook about what to do; it's a feel-your-way-through-it sort of thing.

Though he still had his British accent and proper mannerisms, he didn't really speak like a colonial soldier. His vernacular had clearly changed over the centuries. I looked at Jess. "What else am I supposed to do other than stare at her? She looks so sad and I'm helpless, I can't do anything, she doesn't even know that I am here". He put a calming hand on my shoulder. "She might not be able to see you, but she can feel that you are still here. That is the best you get. You're more of a comfort than anything else, my dear boy. You can't change anything in her life, but you can be there to help her with those moments that try to break you." I remember thinking at the time, that's not good enough! Why can't I change her life? There has to be a way. What is the point of it all if I can't take away her pain? What is the point if I can't help her move on with her life? If I'd only known then how prophetic that thought was and how that idea would eventually change the course of everything for both of us.

I told this to Alistair, but he was no help. I would soon realize this was a pattern with my red-coated friend. I also wanted to understand the ache I kept feeling. All Alistair told me was that those were all good questions and he knew where to get the answers. He took my hand and we left Jess sleeping in her bed. The next thing I knew, we were heading "upstairs".

# 4

# JESS

It had been six months since Jack passed. I finally felt ready to go back to NYU after taking a semester off from film school. When Jack was alive, we used to go to the Film Forum on Saturday nights and watch old movies. One of my favorite dates was when he took me to see The Picture of Dorian Gray, obviously because it was based on the novel by Oscar Wilde. I knew old movies weren't really Jack's thing; he watched them just for me. He thought I never noticed, but he used to spend half the movie watching me enjoy it.

That was Jack, always finding something to enjoy even in things he hated. I loved that about him when he was alive, and I miss that now that he is gone.

I thought about that as I walked back into my first class. The second I walked into my film theory class it just felt wrong. It felt so pointless to me, which was new because it was one of my favorite classes. After everything I had been through recently, just the effort to put on clothes and leave the house was sometimes a struggle. It seemed exhausting to be spending an entire hour discussing some movie from the early 1900s that most people don't even

know exists. It was the opposite of how I used to feel. I could spend hours with my classmates debating what a particular director's vision was or how the choices a cinematographer made in a certain film changed the course of cinema. But now it was altogether uninteresting. I felt lost. For the first time in my life, I didn't know where I was going. I spent most of the day just wandering around the city and I know it sounds ridiculous, but I even said a prayer to Jack in case he was up there watching over me to maybe send me a sign. It was wishful thinking because, of course, I didn't see any signs.

I had made plans to meet up with Andrea for dinner that night. She has become a close friend of mine. After everything, she is the one person who stepped up and was there for me, even on the days I couldn't get out of bed. She would lie in bed with me all day in her pajamas and we would just watch bad movies. I'm so grateful to have her in my life because I know I am not currently the most fun person to be around. We met up at this little tapas place in the West Village off Bleecker Street. She has been forcing me to get out of the house at least once a week.

Honestly, I'd rather just become a full-on agoraphobic hermit and never leave my house, but deep down I know at

some point I am going to need to move on. Jack would want me to move on and be happy.

As I walked into the restaurant, Andrea had already grabbed us a table. She looked stunning as usual. She was half Japanese and had spent a good part of her childhood in Osaka. She is also pretty feisty, and I love that about her. One of my favorite things is to watch a guy hit on her. God forbid they tell her that she looks 'exotic'. She would usually snap back at them some variation of "I'm Japanese, not a unicorn!" It made me laugh every time and right now I needed to laugh more than anything. It turned out to be a pretty fun night. We drank sangria like it was water and laughed nonstop, and not just the polite laugh, but the kind of laugh where your stomach hurts and you're worried that sangria is going to shoot out of your nose. It was nice to feel like I had rejoined the human race for at least an evening. As we were getting ready to leave, that's when it happened—the last moment that changed the course of my life.

Sitting at a nearby table was a nice-looking couple, clearly on a first date from all the fidgeting and awkward smiling they were both doing. As we passed by, I could hear the girl giggling that she had never had escargot before

and wasn't sure how to eat it. I remember chuckling to myself, as I had the same thing happen one night when Jack and I had gone out to dinner. He wasn't sure how to use the little tongs to hold the shell in place and he ended up accidentally flinging the snail across the restaurant. I could see the girl trying to grab the escargot with her fork as we walked out the front door. We hadn't gotten more than three steps outside when we heard screams coming from inside the restaurant.

Andrea and I both turned toward the sound of the screams. When we looked in the window, we could see the girl was now grasping her throat and looking terrified. She was choking. I don't know what came over me, but I dropped my purse and ran back into the restaurant. When I got inside everyone was panicking; no one knew what to do.

Acting on instinct, I ran up behind her and started to do the Heimlich maneuver. I had learned it when I was in school, but I had no idea if I was doing it right or not. All I knew was if no one tried something, this woman would die from trying to impress some guy she may or may not even like. My hands moved around her waist as if on autopilot. I thrust up into her sternum once and nothing happened. She continued to panic and gasp for air. I tightened my grip

around her waist and thrust my hands into her sternum again, harder this time. The next thing I knew, she coughed and spit out the half-eaten piece of escargot and it landed on the table with a squishy thud.

Her date just stood there motionless, unsure what to do. The woman turned to me, still trying to catch her breath, and then she burst into tears and I threw my arms around her. In between her sobs she said, "You saved my life, thank you so much." It was the first time I had hugged someone since Jack died. I felt happy that everything was okay, but I was also a little uncomfortable with the closeness. I wanted to pull away, but I fought the impulse. All I could think about was what I had just done. If I hadn't helped this stranger, she might be dead right now. We all might have been looking at her body slumped over the table. I'd been feeling lost for so long but in that moment I finally felt like something made sense to me. This woman's family wouldn't have to know the pain of losing her they loved. They wouldn't have to feel the pain I was living with. It made me think of Jack. He was the guy who always put other people before himself. He was the consummate gentleman, he held doors for people, helped old ladies across the street, and he would sacrifice just so

other people didn't have to. It made me think, if he were here right now, he would have been proud of me. I smiled to myself. It sounds silly, even now, but I remember in those first months after he passed I was looking for some kind of sign, any sign to tell me what I should do now because no one tells you how to move on from a loss like mine.

It sounds weird but I had this whole life planned with Jack and since he was no longer a part of it, I felt like I'd be cheating on him if I continued on that path. When he was alive, we talked endlessly about how I would finish film school and become some hotshot independent film director and he would travel with me and keep me company.

It was a great dream. But that dream was gone.

As I was saving that woman's life, I knew this was the sign I had been waiting for. Had you told me at the time that a snail would change my life, I would have laughed in your face, but there it was. Saving this woman's life gave me a purpose. I couldn't save Jack but if I could stop someone else from feeling the pain and loss that I felt, then maybe something good could come out of something terrible.

The next day I marched into the administration office at NYU and changed my major to Pre-Med. I would become a
doctor, that way at least I could even the score with death. Death took Jack from me, so I would take people from death.

# 5
# JACK

I don't know what I was expecting when we got to Heaven. I mean, every religion has their different interpretation of Heaven. In Ancient Greece, it was called Elysium and it was reserved for Heroes and for the children of the Gods. In the Hindu religion, Heaven is called Svarga Loka. Over the centuries it has had so many names—Arcadia, Shangri-La, Utopia, the list goes on and on. They usually have similarities though. Heaven is supposed to be paradise. It's your reward for leading a good life on Earth. So, I guess what I was expecting was literally that— paradise. Just beauty as far as the eye could see. I couldn't have been more wrong.

I kid you not, Heaven looks like New York City! It is not what I'd imagined, it's one boring nondescript skyscraper after the next. Where were the rolling hills and the sunshine, hell, where were the fluffy white clouds you dreamed about when you were a kid? Letdown would be an understatement. I honestly thought it was a joke. It looked like we hadn't gone anywhere at all. We could have been on any block in Manhattan and you wouldn't know the

difference. My first questions to Alistair were why does it look like this and how did we get here. I wasn't even sure where 'here' was. Were we above Earth? Or somewhere else entirely? Alistair tried to explain it to me but the idea that humans only use ten percent of their brain is not a joke because it wasn't making much sense. So, he tried a different tack. He said, "Think of it this way. It is as if you are one magnet and Heaven is another magnet. You just have to think about wanting to go to Heaven and the Universe does the rest." I still had no idea what he was talking about, but pretty neat trick, if you asked me. I wondered if that's how it would work with Jess and me. I was already drawn to her, so it made sense that even now, as her Guardian Angel, I still would be.

But I couldn't help thinking that Alistair somehow made a wrong turn somewhere. I remember I looked over at him, confused, and asked, "This...this is Heaven?" He just laughed and said, "It's what you need it to be." One thing about Alistair was he sounded like a fortune cookie half the time. I think he enjoyed it. He usually only made partial sense and it was up to you to figure out the rest. Maybe in time I'd sound wise like that, but in the meantime, it was annoying. I learned later that Heaven

looks like different things to different people. I guess to me it looked like downtown because that was familiar to me. It's an easier transition for humans to see something familiar instead of what Heaven actually looks like. It brings up the question, how can multiple versions of Heaven exist in the same place? The truth is, I have no idea, I guess I would need to use the other ninety percent of my brain to understand that.

We walked for a few minutes, heading towards one of the taller buildings. The only thing that stood out to me was that there was no one around. The whole "Heavenly" city was quiet, no people, no cars, no Angels. The silence was piercing. Take a walk one day through Central Park at dawn and stick your fingers in your ears to drown out all the sounds of nature, and you'll get an idea of how eerily quiet it was. We arrived at the tallest building of the bunch and went inside. We hopped in the elevator and there were no buttons of any kind. The walls were sleek and metallic. I asked Alistair where we were heading. He just smiled and waved his hand over the blank wall and a button with a symbol I didn't recognize appeared. He pressed the button and the elevator started heading up. After what felt

like an eternity the elevator stopped, and the doors opened, and we got out.

The floor we were on was absolutely massive. The building was like the TARDIS—you know, bigger on the inside than on the outside. And there were people mingling around, finally. Well, I guess they were technically all Angels; I wasn't sure. Alistair, with all the flair he could muster with his British accent, announced, "Welcome to Heaven!" Whomp, whomp. I couldn't help feeling disappointed. There were no pearly white gates. Nothing. But maybe it was all me. Alistair said Heaven is what we need it to be.

Apparently I needed a lawyer because it looked more like I was at a law firm waiting for a job interview. He gave me the tour as we walked. He gestured to the left. "Over that way is for New Arrivals, the souls that have just crossed over and are being 'processed', as they like to call it." We continued on and he gestured to the right down a long hallway. "And down there is Human Resources." I looked back at him and smirked. "Heaven has an HR department?"

"It's a bit different than your Human Resources, my young friend. That is where the records on every human on the planet are, their birth, their life, their death, whether those events have happened yet or not."

I stopped Alistair. "Wait, you know when people are going to die? What about free will and all that?" He patted me on the head like I was a child and said, "Free will is an illusion. It is something humans created to help them deal with a world they have no control over. Fate exists for a reason. The world exists in a very delicate balance. The world below and the world above co-exist and without that balance there would be chaos. Every moment of every life is in that room. Why do you think everything is so calm around here? Imagine seven billion lives on Earth. What if there were no plan for any of them? The world and everything in it would crumble, so yes, fate exists as a sort of checks-and-balances on existence." I thought about this for a second and then something occurred to me. I asked him, "Does this mean you knew that the day I ran to the bodega I was going to die?" Alistair paused. He didn't say a word, but his eyes spoke volumes. I know he had told me Guardian Angels don't feel, but I don't know how true that was, because I remember, in that moment I was so angry I could barely see straight.

I grabbed him by his stupid red coat. "How could you not tell me, warn me, something, so I could prepare, so I could tell Jess! So I could say goodbye! How can you just let her suffer like that?" He pulled my hands off of his coat and calmly said, "We can't, Jack. That is not how it works. No matter how much I may have wanted to tell you, we can't, it is forbidden, we can't interfere in the course of a human life. There are consequences." I was still fuming. "What kind of consequences?" He looked at me and in total seriousness replied, "The end of existence." Existence was not what I was thinking about. I was only thinking about Jess. I could have hugged her one last time. I could have kissed her goodbye. I didn't understand why there were all these rules. It just wasn't fair. I calmed myself down. "But is it possible? COULD you have warned me?" He put his hand on my cheek like a dad does with his son when he gets a skinned knee and smiled. "Everything is possible Jack, however unlikely, or improbable." I rolled my eyes at him. Great, more fortune-cookie talk.

We moved on down the hallway towards a big set of wooden doors. Once we got close enough Alistair waved his hands and a placard appeared next to the door. It read, "Guardian Angels for Dummies". I glared over at Alistair and he just smirked. Is it possible for a Guardian Angel to be an asshole?

We walked through the doors and into a giant empty white room. I looked over at him, confused, as I often did— no wonder he thinks I'm clueless. And as I looked back, the room started to change. Bookshelves materialized from the walls, a large desk with a lamp appeared in the center of the room. Alistair walked over to the bookshelf. "On these shelves you will find everything that you need to know about being a Guardian Angel, everyone that has come before you. Everything we can do, and cannot do, it is all here. I suggest you get to reading, unless you want to spend the rest of eternity sitting in a chair and staring at Jess like some sort of cretin." Yep, it's definitely possible for a Guardian Angel to be an asshole!

I went over to the first bookshelf and grabbed the first book I saw. The title was "Angels: A History"; I flipped it open and started reading. It was fascinating and a little shocking how much the Bible had gotten wrong. With every book I picked up, there were more and more things I noticed that various religions had gotten wrong. The main takeaway I had was that no one religion had gotten it 'right'. Basically, it is the Golden Rule that you should follow. Essentially, treat people how you would want to be treated and you should be all right. And the occasional prayer doesn't hurt either. I continued to read but I also had other things on my mind. I didn't tell Alistair, but there was only one thing I wanted to learn—how to communicate with Jess. That was my one goal, to let her know I was there and she would be all right, to let her know it was okay to move on. And with that in mind, I set out to read everything in the library.

Remember when I told you time works differently for Guardian Angels? It only took me a few weeks to read everything in the entire room. I must have read a thousand books. I had nothing but time on my hands. Guardian Angels don't need to eat or sleep, so day and night I read and read; the more I read, the more I understood what I was and what I could do. I learned that it is possible to affect the human world. Guardian Angels can't reach out and turn off a light switch or anything like that. We cannot affect anything with a physical form. We can't touch or move anything with mass. But we can affect things in the natural world, we aren't entirely helpless. For example, we can make the breeze blow stronger, we can make sunlight appear brighter. The more I read things like that, the more I realized it might be hard but I could at least try and communicate with Jess. We can affect the world around us,

but humans cannot see, hear, nor touch us. It's one of those rules to keep a balance in the world, to prevent existence from crumbling. I hated it, but it did make sense. Think about how many humans lose their mind when they think they see Bigfoot or the Loch Ness Monster or something they can't grasp. How would the world react if they knew for a fact there were Angels and Guardian Angels, among other things, around them all the time? It is one thing to believe in the idea of something, it's another thing to know for a fact that it's a reality. How long before they thought they were surrounded by Demons too, and the world descended into chaos?

Amongst my reading I came across a book that piqued my interest called "Facets of Humanity: From the Earthly Plane and Beyond". For the first time in what felt like weeks, the second I held that book the ache in my chest lessened. I had hope. While Alistair was gone, I quickly read the book. It detailed all the ways mankind exists between the worlds of the living and the dead, whether it be through spiritual meditation, near-death experience, or simply by accident. One of the stories was an account of a Guardian Angel possessing a human in order to return to physical form. So, it is possible to come back! The more I read

though, the more my hopes sank, and I could see why Alistair had told me it was impossible to return. I'll just say that things did not end well for that particular Guardian Angel. While the story was clearly meant as a parable and a warning to not go outside the accepted order of things, there still remained a tiny glimmer of hope.

Obviously, I was not going to do what this Guardian Angel had done, but maybe there was something else I could do to talk to Jess. Maybe there was some loophole I could find. It was a longshot, but it was something.

Once I finished reading that book it was time to get back to Jess. I had no idea how long I was gone but I knew that I needed to get back. Alistair said I needed to give her time to grieve, that it was all part of the healing process. But a few weeks was enough time I felt, so I headed back.

# 6

# JESS

Time is supposed to heal all wounds. That is what they say, right? If it didn't, and we were meant to feel the raw pain that immediately accompanies loss for the rest of our lives, it would be too much for most people. It is supposed get easier the more distance you have from whatever happened to you. There are a million sayings for it—just hang in there, this too shall pass. At Jack's funeral, my older relatives and family friends told me all of those things, those empty sentiments. That may have been the case for them, but it hasn't really worked out that way for me. It's been eight years today since that day at the bodega and it still feels like it happened yesterday. If I close my eyes, I can still smell the pasta burnt on the stove.

Nothing from that day feels any easier. If anything, the pain is worse. The world just feels empty, lonely, not as bright as it used to, without Jack in it.

Every year on the anniversary of his death I make the same meal I made on that day and I take it to the cemetery and spend the day with him. It sounds morbid but it's the closest I can get to being with him. So just like I had

 done for the past seven years, I packed up a picnic basket and headed out to the cemetery where we buried Jack. It was always the best day of the year. For one day a year, I don't have to deal with people looking at me with those sad eyes. They think I don't see it, when my co-workers look at me like I'm that broken girl who hasn't gotten back out there yet. I know they mean well and it's only because they care, but after this long those looks just irritate me.

I mean, technically they are right. I haven't been on a date since Jack, but what's the point? He was my other half; I'm never going to find that again. Love like that doesn't come along twice in a lifetime. Lightning doesn't strike twice; neither does love. Besides, I'm so busy with the last couple years of my residency that I don't really have time to date anyway. Or at least that's what I tell myself when the loneliness hits particularly hard.

It was a beautiful fall day in New York, the leaves were just starting to turn, and it was cool but not too cold. We buried Jack in Green-Wood Cemetery in Brooklyn. The thing about cemeteries is, of course they are sad, but they are also beautiful. I guess the logic is you are going there for such a terrible reason you might as well have something beautiful to look at. The other thing about cemeteries is that you don't have to put on airs. You get to just feel whatever you want to feel. You don't have to pretend you aren't sad. You don't have to pretend you aren't broken. Everyone there is going through or has gone through exactly what you have been through so it's a safe place to just be. However, you grieve, whether it's hysterical crying or just silence, no one is ever going to judge you or give you that pitying look. I liked that.

I got out of the cab and walked through the park to get to his gravesite. I always get butterflies as I come over that last hill. I don't know why, I guess the dreamer in me thinks that maybe, one day, he'll be there waiting on the other side of the hill. He never is, of course, but sure enough as I came to that last hill the familiar twinge started in my stomach. Most years there are a few people mingling around off in the distance, but not today; today it was just Jack and me. I spent the first few minutes cleaning up. The groundskeepers do a good job of keeping everything tidy, but I like to give his headstone a good polish. It makes me feel like I am somehow taking care of him, just like when I would iron his shirts for him so he wouldn't look like a wrinkled mess all the time. He still often did. It's funny the memories you hold onto. No matter

how much I ironed his clothes, he would always end up wrinkled five minutes after he got dressed. I laid out the picnic, one setting for me and one for Jack, and I sat and faced him—well...his headstone.

I took a sip of wine. "So my second year of residency is going pretty well. Do you remember that doctor I told you about? Dr. Anderson? Well he has taken me on as a mentee, so I think I'm going to be an ER doctor. Pretty cool, right?" It just felt natural to talk to him as if he were there. After everything I said I would always pause and think of what his response would be; he'd say "J, that's amazing, I'm so proud of you!" J was his pet name for me. I kind of hated it, it made me sound like a boy, but it's what he would have said. And I would carry on like that till I ran out of things to talk about and that's when the sadness would kick in because if Jack were really there, the conversation would never end. He could talk the ears off of anyone; he just had that gift. Everyone he met, no matter where, no matter who they were, they were instantly his best friend. I used to get annoyed when he would talk to everyone at the grocery store. We would always end up taking way longer than we needed to. But I

would happily spend hours talking to every stranger on the street just to have him by my side again.

The saddest part of the day would be when the sun started to set and I had to start packing up the picnic basket. Picking up "his" plate, still full of pasta, always choked me up. But despite the moments of sadness,

## JESS

it is and will always be a day I look forward to every year.

# 7

# JACK

When I got back to Earth, I was outside of our apartment. It had been close to a month, or at least that was my best guess; there are no clocks in Heaven. But something felt different. I couldn't feel Jess, not like I could during my funeral, not like I could when I was watching her grieve. I looked at Alistair but he couldn't meet my eyes—or didn't want to. Where was Jess? Why couldn't I feel her presence? How was I going to find her? Then I realized I knew exactly how to find her. I remembered what Alistair told me about magnets and the pull between Guardian Angels and Heaven. And after reading everything in the library I knew my theory about the connection between Jess and me was also true. As her Guardian Angel, I simply had to concentrate on her and the magnetic forces would bring me to her. I closed my eyes and focused. When I opened them, I was at New York General Hospital. Jess was here. Had something happened to her while I was gone? Was she ill? I walked from floor to floor and I felt her presence grow stronger and stronger as I entered the ICU wing.

Oh God, I would never forgive myself if I let something happen to her. But who am I kidding, it's not like I would have been able to do anything to stop whatever happened to her. For a moment, I felt like maybe it was for the best. If she crossed over then we would be together again. Selfishly, I didn't hate the prospect of that, assuming nothing painful happened to her. As I walked down the hall, I looked in all the rooms, but she was nowhere to be found. I reached the end of the corridor and looked up at the sign on the door. It read "Surgery". Jess was in there.

Ache...

While the selfish part of me wanted her with me, the majority of me just wanted her to be safe, even if that meant we couldn't be together. I instinctively clutched my chest, closed my eyes, and said a prayer. I walked through the doors. I could feel Jess. She was in the last operating room on the right. I walked slower than I realized. The thing with Guardian Angels is, we may not have the requisite parts anymore, but it doesn't mean we are incapable of feelings or emotions. We feel differently, deeper. We feel with our entire souls. It's hard to quantify just how it all works. Oh god, I'm beginning to

sound like Alistair. Is that what is going to happen to me? In two hundred years, will I become an Angelic Douchebag? I was afraid to look in through the observation window for fear of what I might see, but I had to know, I had to know what happened to Jess, what happened to my love, my soul, my everything.

I looked in and there was a woman on the table, but it was not Jess. It was an elderly woman. I felt Jess's soul in this room but she was not here. That is when I saw her. She wasn't on the table. She was standing over the woman holding a suction tube while the surgeon worked on the elderly woman's internal organs. What was happening?

Alistair came up and stood next to me. "Jack, there is something you need to understand. Do you remember how I told you time works differently for Guardian Angels?" I nodded yes, and he continued, "Well, time works differently between the planes of Heaven and Earth as well."

"What does that even mean, Alistair? Enough with the riddles, how long have we been gone?" Alistair lowered his head, "We've been gone for eight years."

Ache...

How could eight years have passed? We were only gone for a few weeks, a month, tops. What kind of Guardian Angel was I? I had left her alone for eight years! The hollowness grew inside me.

Ache...

What kind of Guardian Angel was I if the one person I was supposed to be looking after has been without me for so long? How could Alistair not have told me this would happen? When I left, she was finishing up her film degree at NYU. I had always believed Jess would be one of the success stories. She and I both knew how hard it would be to become a success in the film industry but, call it intuition, I never doubted for a second that she would be one of the ones who "made it". How had her life changed so much?

I stood there watching her work for hours. It was like I was seeing a completely different person. A person I didn't know. This person was not my Jess. She was so precise, so mechanical, so clinical in her movements. After the surgery, I followed her back to the residents' locker room. She grabbed her bag and a few things from her locker. As she was getting ready to leave a few more doctors came into the locker room. A blond-haired doctor asked Jess to join them for a drink. Jess barely even acknowledged their presence and dismissed their invitation with a quiet "no thanks" as she walked out of the room. Once Jess was gone, a brunette doctor asked the blond doctor, "Why do you even bother with her? She never wants to join the group." The blonde replied sadly, "I don't know, I guess I just feel bad for her, you know she has no friends. I'm just hoping that one of these days she will say yes. No one should be alone all the time, that's no way to live." The brunette just rolled her eyes and started getting undressed.

## JACK

My worst fear came true. The day I died was the day Jess stopped living. The girl who could light up a room with her mere presence was gone. All I saw now was a shell. It looked and sounded like Jess but it was just a vessel.

She was a Russian nesting doll with no other dolls hidden within her.

I walked behind Jess as she left the hospital and got on the subway. She barely made eye contact with people, choosing to just stare down at a medical journal as she took the train downtown to the West Village. She made a quick stop to grab some takeout and then she went home.

When we got back to her apartment the silence was deafening. When we were together there was always noise coming from our apartment, whether it was some crazy conversation that was generally just our version of

foreplay or Jess blasting old records. She used to say that music died with the invention of the CD, that the only way to record music was on vinyl because it captured all the imperfections and that's what made it perfect.

Honestly, I couldn't care less about records versus CDs, but Jess was as passionate about music as she was about film. But that's not who Jess is now. Her apartment was antiseptic. It was clinical. There was no life, no light here. Everything was immaculate. I felt like I didn't know who this person was. How could she have changed so much? She put her bag and coat in her closet, grabbed an unopened bottle of wine from the fridge, and sat down on the couch with a glass. She grabbed the remote and turned on the television and the DVD player. When she pressed play on the DVD it all made sense.

I saw myself on the screen. It was from happier times obviously. It was a home movie of the party we threw after I had proposed to Jess. On the screen, as I talked about the reasons why I wanted to spend the rest of my life with her, she sat on the couch and whispered what I was saying in perfect unison. How many times had she watched this?

More times than she would like to admit to herself, I would imagine. Back on the screen I continued to rattle off sarcastically all the things I loved about Jess, like her love of bad 80s horror movies, the way she uses her finger to clean a plate of food she liked when she thinks no one is looking. But then I got serious. "And to quote our dear friend Oscar Wilde, to live is the rarest thing in the world, most people exist, that is all." Onscreen, Jess snuck up behind me, clearly tipsy, and replied with our special line, "And what is rarer still is to love without boundaries," and then planted a big sloppy chardonnay-infused kiss on me. As we kissed on the screen, Jess paused the TV right as our lips met. She put down the remote, downed her full glass of chardonnay and began to cry.

As she sobbed on the couch, I once again felt the familiar helplessness I had felt those first few days after I died.

Ache...

I tried to focus and think about everything I had read. What could I do to make her feel my presence, to show her I was there? I focused on the air coming from the air conditioner. I focused all of me on it. I was able to briefly make the air flow faster. She didn't even notice.

She was too wrapped up in her tears. Is this what she did every night? What kind of a life is that? I tried to touch her shoulder, but my hand passed through her like I was made of nothing. I was made of nothing to her. In that moment, I don't know who was emptier—Jess or I.

My mind drifted to the book I had read in the stacks in Heaven called "Facets of Humanity: From the Earthly Plane and Beyond". I remembered the story of the Guardian Angel who had possessed a human. I remembered the severity of the consequences of his actions. I thought to myself, there has to be a way to do that without the repercussions. There had to be some kind of loophole. But how was I going to figure that out? I was a brand-new Guardian Angel. If no one had figured out a way around this in the entire course of human history, what hope did I have? Then it hit me— Human Resources! Alistair told me that they keep track of all life and ALL DEATH. The story I read back in the library about the Guardian Angel being punished was because it had happened when the human still had a soul. Maybe that was the problem, occupying a vessel that was already occupied.

Maybe the loophole is finding an unoccupied vessel?

But how was I going to find a person who had no soul? I did have an idea, though it was beyond crazy. But it might just be crazy enough to work. If I found a person who was about

to pass, maybe I could take over their body when their soul left it. That way it wouldn't really be possession, because their soul would have moved on. It was more like borrowing an empty body. Could that work? Would the consequences be the same? I had no idea, but I had to give it a shot. I looked at Jess. "Hang on, Jess, I'm coming." Not that she could hear me.

# 8

# JESS

I was getting ready to finish up my rounds. It had been a long night and not a particularly pleasant one. The hardest part of being a doctor is being the one who has to tell people their loved ones have passed or, even worse, that they aren't going to make it. I know what it feels like to have your whole world crumble from one second to the next. You hope the days you save your patients far outweigh days like today. To watch that realization come across people's faces never gets easier. And no two people react the same way. Sometimes people just collapse in a sobbing heap as if their bodies can't physically sustain the news, but what is even worse are the people who take a while to comprehend it. It's like their minds can't process the information so it just gets dismissed. That happened last night with one of my patients, a young man, not much older than I was, named Eric Frasier. From what his family had told me, Eric was their pride and joy, their only child. Eric had been injured in a skiing accident. As he was coming down the mountain, he lost control and ended up rolling down the hill and landing in a pile of fresh snow,

unconscious and upside down. By the time his friends reached him he had been without oxygen for several minutes. He had been in the ICU for two weeks now. We had been running tests daily to see if there was any brain activity, but there never was. The only thing keeping him alive was the machines he was hooked up to. For all intents and purposes, Eric was already gone. He was brain dead. But his family clung to hope that he might pull through. You could almost see that hope rise and fall as his heartbeat hit peaks and valleys on the nearby machine. But it was artificial hope. The only things causing that heartbeat were the machines. Without them he would expire.

I had a meeting with my mentor, Dr. Anderson to discuss what to do next, if there was anything to do at all. We went through his chart one final time and we both concluded that there was nothing more we could do for Eric. It was time to tell his family that Eric would never recover.

As I walked down the hallway to meet his parents, my feet felt like lead, like they were stuck in quicksand and the closer I got to them the deeper and more treacherous it became. Part of me thought, if only the quicksand were real, then I wouldn't have to destroy this family. But I had no choice it is part of the job. As I turned the corner, I saw his parents. His mom, Betty, was sitting there clutching her purse, her pink pastel shawl draped softly over her ample shoulders. Her hair was teased within an inch of its life but that was the style du jour in their modest Midwestern town. She had told me during one of our conversations that she had faith Eric was going to get better because she had known deep down in her heart she was going to be a grandmother someday, and seeing as Eric was her only child, she had been praying and believed God would not take her Eric so soon. I had come to learn she was a deeply religious woman who believed in the power of prayer to heal almost anything. Eric's father Bob, who had strong hands and the weathered skin of a farmer, was even more sure his son would pull through because he had always managed to overcome adversity when he was a kid.

How was I supposed to tell these nice people that all their hopes and dreams for their future and for their son's future were over? I've never been a religious person, so I never understood the people who would pray to God and feel like he answered them. I never passed judgment but given what I have been through in my life, I don't believe whatever God you believe in has any say in what happens in

a life. We are all just passing through and we cling to whatever we can to help us understand this world, or to find a little piece of happiness in the world amongst all the chaos and the horrible things that happen daily. I realize that is a pretty pessimistic and cynical worldview. I didn't always believe that, I used to be a more optimistic person, a more spiritual person, but we change as a result of the experiences we are forced to go through and what I went through after losing Jack changed me. I no longer had the hope I once did. How could I believe in a world, in a Heaven that would take away the one thing that meant more to me than anything? It's not like I am jaded or anything like that, there is still joy and happiness in the world and I believe in that and I hope I find it again someday, but it will never be Jack or what I had with him. I just think the world is a shade gloomier without him in it. But I had to forget all that because what I had to do wasn't about me; it was about Betty and Bob and what I had to help them understand.

I didn't want to crush their world, but there was no choice, Eric was never coming back. I walked into his hospital room, he looked the same, nothing had changed. As I got closer Betty stood up and gave me a big hug. She and

I had grown closer since we had conversations every time I went to check on Eric. She had the warmth I wished my own mother had a little bit more of. We are trained that as doctors we have to do our best to not get attached to patients, or the families of patients, because then we would be devastated every time we lost a patient. But we are all still humans and I just couldn't be that way, that clinical. Betty had joked that she was going to try and set me up with Eric when he got better. She would say I am too pretty of a girl to be single and too serious for my own good. She was right, about the latter. She did make me laugh and I would be lying if I said I hadn't had a dream or two that Eric came out of everything and took me out on a date and was everything Betty told me he was. But that just isn't reality—well...not the reality for Betty and Bob, anyway.

I sat down in the empty chair near them. Betty looked at me cheerfully. "And how is my boy doing today? He looks like he has more color in his cheeks." I tried to smile, but I honestly don't think I could have made my face muscles move, at least not in the direction of a smile. I took a deep breath. "Betty, there hasn't been any change in Eric's vitals and the last EEG we did showed no significant brain activity. I'm afraid the time has come to talk about what to do." Betty just smiled at me clearly not understanding where the conversation was going. "Yes, Dr. Miller, what is the next step? I just want to make sure we are doing everything the right way so when Eric wakes up there aren't any complications." I reached out and took her hand in mine. "Betty, Eric isn't going to wake up." I looked over at Bob and I could see on his face that he understood what I was saying. The tears started to well up in his eyes. Betty put her hand on my cheek. "Don't be silly, Dr. Miller, Eric is going to come out of this and be better than ever. Look at all the machines, they are all beeping exactly as they have been since we got here." As I looked back to Betty she had the same maternal smile I had looked forward to seeing every morning when I did my rounds. "I know, Betty. What those machines and the tests we ran are telling us is that Eric is brain dead, there is nothing more we can do for him, he isn't going to get better. I'm afraid the time has come to discuss what kind of future Eric can really have. I took a look at his medical records and Eric has signed a DNR, do you know what that means?" Betty stared at me blankly, but the smile was gone, it was slowly starting to sink in. I fumbled with the

file I was holding in my hand "DNR stands for 'Do Not Resuscitate'. It means Eric wished to not be brought back by CPR if there was a serious accident. The local hospital that treated him prior to his transfer here did not know that and hooked him up to all these machines. We have done everything within our power to try and bring him back, but nothing has worked. I'm so sorry. We need to discuss what Eric would have wanted."

Betty instinctively reached over and grabbed Bob's hand. It had finally sunk in what we were discussing. Bob cleared his throat. "So what are you saying, Dr. Miller, are you asking if we should turn off Eric's machines? What do you think we should do?" As doctors, we have all been through extensive training to deal with situations like this, but they never really prepare you for how horrible it feels to tell someone that it's up to them to decide what to do. "I'm afraid I can't answer that, Mr. Frasier, Bob."

The truth is that Eric is beyond our help and without these machines keeping him alive, Eric will pass. Since he signed a DNR we know Eric would not have wanted to be in this position, but unfortunately these are the circumstances we are in. I am so very sorry." Betty looked at me, tears streaming down her face. "How am I supposed to say goodbye to Eric? You're asking us to kill our son." I took Betty's hand. "No, Betty, Eric's body may be lying in that bed, but the Eric you know and love is not there anymore, and nothing we do will change that." Betty just continued to cry, Bob looked up and met my eyes. "Can we have a little time? Do we need to decide right now?" I told him they should take some time and really think about Eric's wishes. As I walked down the hall, I could still hear Betty crying. I went into the stairwell I knew was hardly ever used and I began to sob.

## 9

## JACK

When I got back to the "familiar" empty urban landscape of Heaven I still didn't have a game plan yet. I knew I needed to get back to Jess and the best way to do that was to find something or someone, somewhere in the Human Resources department who for lack of a better term was getting close to kicking the bucket. I know how cavalier this all sounds but if what Alistair had told me was accurate, then there was nothing to stop someone from passing on. So, it's not like I am ending someone's life early. I am just taking advantage of a situation that is already happening. And truth be told, I may not even be able to do anything, but I had to at least try. I couldn't spend another day watching what had become of Jess, I just couldn't let go of the image of her sitting alone watching old home movies of us. This isn't a life. If I had really been gone for eight years, she had grieved for me long enough. I won't lie, there was a part of me that was thankful she hadn't just forgotten about me and moved on with the first guy who paid her some attention. But if you love someone you want the best for them, even if the best for them isn't you. It was time for her to move on.

I walked and walked until I reached the building Alistair had brought me to when we first arrived in Heaven. I got in the elevator and waved my arm just as he did previously, and just as before a small button, with the same symbol, appeared. I pressed it and the elevator rocketed upwards. When the doors opened, I started making my way towards the hallway where Alistair had pointed to the Human Resources sign. I was about to turn down the hallway when I heard a voice behind me. "Is there something I can help you with?" I turned around to see a mousy older woman at the end of the hallway. Was she a Guardian Angel, or something else? She looked like my Aunt Esther, whose dentures were so big it looked like she was always trying to eat her own head. I tried to think about what I should do; I hadn't really taken into account that I might not just be able to walk right into Human Resources. If I lied, would she know I was lying? Can I even lie anymore? Is there a Guardian Angel lie detector test? There was only one way to find out. I turned around towards her and put on the biggest, least fake looking smile I could muster. "I'm so sorry, I'm new here and I'm sort of lost, can you help

me find Human Resources?" It wasn't technically a lie. She was also much younger than my Aunt Esther and denture free. The woman hesitated for a moment and then broke out into a smile. "Well, why didn't you say so in the first place, darling? I must have mixed up the days, you weren't supposed to be joining us for another couple of days." Her accent was hard to place, but she sounded Scandinavian, if I had to hazard a guess. She didn't look much older than late 40s but in Heaven everything is about perception; for all I know she could be thousands of years old. I might be talking to an actual Viking.

We walked in relative silence towards the Human Resources office. As we entered the room looked entirely empty, save for two desks and at one of them sat an elderly man. "Hello there, Ainsley," said the woman escorting me.

He looked up at us as we entered. "Good afternoon, Brigida, what can

I do for you?" She gestured to me. "Here is the new guy you requested; he is a bit early." Ainsley looked me up and down and then turned his gaze to Brigida. "He most certainly is not, Brigida. As you well know, I am expecting a woman, now what is her name?" He started to shuffle through the piles of papers on his desk. I thought to myself, I'm done for, he is going to find this other

person's name, and then what will happen to me? I can't imagine lying in Heaven is a good thing, but I had come too far now to not at least try and smooth things over. I cleared my throat. "He is actually correct, Brigida, you were originally supposed to have someone else, but they made some changes and now you have me." Ainsley looked very annoyed. "And WHO made these changes?" I hesitated for a second and then did the only thing that popped into my head. I reached out my hand and pointed upwards. Ainsley and then Brigida followed my hand up to where I was pointing, and then they shared a look but said nothing.

Ainsley stood up and adjusted his trousers. "Very well. My good man, would you please wait here while I go upstairs and sort things out? Thank you, Brigida, I will take it from here." There was an undertone of anger in his voice, but he was covering it with civility, barely. They both walked out together leaving me alone in the Human Resources office. Here was probably the only chance I was going to get because no doubt once they went "upstairs" they would find out I was lying and most likely I would end up "downstairs" for a long time. I mean thou shalt not lie is one of the freaking commandments! But maybe the punishment

wouldn't be that severe. It was just a little white lie. Maybe they grade on a curve?

As soon as they were out of the room I ran over to the desk and looked through the pile of papers on it. There was no rhyme or reason to any of it. I also couldn't read them. They might as well have been written in Greek. It looked vaguely similar to the writing on the button in the elevator. I guess this is the language of the Angels? So Brigida and Ainsley were definitely older than they appeared. Where is Google Translate when you need it? Maybe in time I will know what this all says. I wonder when I'm supposed to learn that? I looked around the room and there was nothing, just empty walls. It made no sense, there had to be filing cabinets or a computer or something. If what Alistair told me was true there couldn't just be nothing, there had to be some sort of record on all the souls on Earth, there just had to be, or this whole plan was for nothing. I ran over to the walls and started waving my arms, hoping that just like in the elevator something would appear, a door, a filing cabinet, anything. I checked the first wall and nothing, the second and still nothing. When I got to the final wall, I closed my eyes and pictured a door and waved my arm and sure enough a door appeared. It

was made of very old wood with a large lock that required one of those keys you would find in a Victorian home. I tried to turn the knob, but it was locked. Where was I supposed to get a key? I looked back at the desk realizing it was the only place a key could possibly be—that is, unless Ainsley had it in his pocket.

I opened the top drawer of the desk and there was a ring of at least forty keys. Every key looked nearly identical. This was going to take forever, and I had considerably less time than forever before I was caught. I grabbed it and ran back over to the door and started trying every key. The longer I kept trying to get the door open the less time I would have to find what I was looking for and I only had one shot at this. It's not like I could pretend to be someone else again and sneak back in here.

The first eleven keys did not unlock the door. I tried the twelfth key, nothing, sixteenth key nothing, thirty-fourth key and still nothing. I was down to only two keys I hadn't tried. I slid the second to last key in the lock and it turned, I had found the right key! I stepped back and I could hear a series of heavy locks clicking and moving behind the door. Much like the rest of Heaven things weren't what they appeared, and this door was more than

just a regular door, it sounded like it was a safe unlocking. Once the sound stopped, I took the handle and turned it and pushed the door open.

When I stepped inside my momentary jubilation disappeared. As far as I could see were hundreds, thousands of shelves all packed with boxes and files. I had maybe five minutes at most before they came back. I had five minutes to search through a room the size of a stadium. It was hopeless, but I had come too far now to give up. I might never have another chance. The room looked like a giant cavern that would have existed under a medieval castle. Gone were all the mod-cons of the Human Resources office. The room had a dank smell, the air felt damp and there was a slight odor of mold wafting through. There were no lights, but rather fires burned along the walls casting a soft glow around the room. I went over to the first stack of files and opened them. I was unable to read them. In my frustration, I muttered to myself, "Why can't these be in English?" I had barely finished my sentence when the images on the pages started to rearrange themselves. Slowly I was able to read them, they were in English now. Pretty nifty trick I thought. I flipped through the first file and it was about a person who had died almost 800 years ago.

How was this vault organized? There had to be some rhyme or reason to it. Was it alphabetical? By date of birth? Of death? I put the file back and ran over to the next shelf and grabbed a file. It was about a woman who had died 650 years ago. I didn't have time to check more files, so I just guessed. Hopefully they were organized by date of death. I ran in the direction of where I thought the most recently deceased files would be stored. I hoped that once I got to those, the next shelves over were for people who were going to pass soon. I could be wrong, those files could be in a completely different room, but I was almost out of time. As I ran from shelf to shelf, I saw that the files began to look less and less tattered and it gave me hope that I had made the right decision. I reached the last shelf of files and started looking through them.

It turns out I was right; this last shelf was for souls that had not passed over yet but would soon enough. The first file I found was for a young boy in Palestine who would be killed tomorrow in a bombing. The next file was for a 102-year-old woman in Northern Scotland who was going to die in 4 days from natural causes. I kept flipping through files, faster and faster. A man in Nigeria...no.

Twins from Paris who will die during childbirth...no. I was running out of hope when I found what I was looking for. He had suffered brain damage in an accident and was set to cross over tomorrow, and he was in New York, it was perfect! I looked at the name on the file: Eric Frasier.

# 10

# JESS

I got the call late last night. After they'd had some time to think about it, Betty and Bob had decided it was time to say goodbye to Eric. It was Bob who called me; I don't think Betty had the strength to say the words out loud and I can't say I blame her. It was still hard for me to say, to this day, that Jack was dead. We made arrangements for the next day to meet at the hospital. I woke up with a sadness that felt even more profound than what I was used to. It made me think of Jack and what I would have done had he survived but ended up on life support. Would I have been able to turn the machines off? I don't know that I would have been able to say goodbye like that. I don't know if I would have been able to look him in the eyes and watch the life drain out of them. It sounds horrible to say but I was grateful that when Jack was shot he passed quickly. I know Jack wouldn't have wanted to live hooked up to machines, but would I have had the strength to end his life? Thankfully I will never know the answer to that question.

Getting out of bed was a struggle, more so than usual.

I just kept picturing Betty's eyes red from tears. I made my usual cup of coffee and tried to force myself to eat something as I finished getting ready to head to the hospital. I was in a daze I couldn't snap out of, but I had to. I already knew in my gut that Betty and Bob were going to need me to be the strong one, they were going to need my help so they could say goodbye to Eric. I must have zoned out because 20 minutes went by in a flash and I was running late. I poured the rest of my coffee into my travel mug, grabbed my bag and ran out the door. I walked up to Christopher Street and hopped on the subway to head to the hospital. I got there just as Betty and Bob were walking in. Betty gave me a big hug, like I was her daughter who was just coming home from her first semester at college.

Don't get attached, I kept telling myself, don't get attached. But how could I not? I'm not a robot, even if some of the other residents think I am. This day was always going to be the worst day of Betty and Bob's lives. The least I could do was to try to make it just a little bit easier for them.

The first thing they had to do was fill out a lot of paperwork. Bob filled out most of it, Betty just sat quietly by his side clutching her purse. Once all of that was taken care of, we went up to Eric's room so they could spend some time with him. Betty did the same thing she had done every single time she showed up to the hospital. She pulled a small brush out of her purse and combed Eric's hair, so it looked as neat as possible. When she finished, she smoothed out his sheets and tucked them in on the sides. Every time she did that it made me think of how when I was a little girl my dad used to tuck me into bed. He would tuck the sheets in so tight around me and he used to joke that I was his favorite little burrito.

Betty sat down next to Bob and they both looked at me.

Betty finally spoke, "Now what?" I tried to sound as professional as possible, but inside I just kept saying to myself, don't cry, don't cry. I took a deep breath. "Well, that depends on you. If there is anything else you want to say to Eric, now would be the time, otherwise we can get started." It was then that Bob's strength left him. He tried to speak but choked on his words, "What will happen?" I looked them both in the eyes. "Well, the first thing I will do is turn off his respirator, which is the machine helping him breathe. Then I will remove the wires monitoring his pulse. And then we wait for Eric to..." I

hesitated, trying to think of the right word to say, but the truth is there are no right or wrong words in a situation like this. "We wait for Eric to move on." Betty lowered her head and stared at her purse. "Will it hurt? Is he in pain?" I sat down next to Betty and I took her hand. "I can assure you Eric is not in any pain." Betty continued, "But what if he wakes up, what if there's been a mistake, how can we be sure we are doing the right thing?" Bob put his hands in hers. "Betty, this is what Eric would have wanted, he wouldn't want a life like this." You always hope that, as a couple, you learn to work as a team. Those are the couples who last. When one of you is weak, the other is strong. I knew Jack and I would be that kind of couple. Seeing Betty and Bob interact, it's no wonder they had been married for over forty years. Betty put her head on his shoulder and began to cry again. "You have to do it, I don't think I can."

Bob stood up, still holding Betty's hand, "Okay, Dr. Miller it's time, what do I have to do?" I brought Bob closer to Eric's bed. The respirator was moving up and down and made a steady whooshing sound as it fed oxygen through the tube in Eric's mouth into his lungs. The sensors monitoring his pulse continued to steadily beat in a sinus rhythm. I talked Bob through what he would need to do. He let go of Betty's hand and walked closer to Eric's bed.

He looked at me for reassurance. I squeezed his hand. "Is there anything you want to say to Eric?" Bob just nodded softly, leaned down close to Eric, and spoke softly, "Goodbye, my beautiful boy, thank you for blessing our lives for as long as you did. Please don't worry, your mother and I will get through this. And even though we will be apart for now, we will all be together soon enough in Heaven. You rest now." Bob turned back to Betty. "Do you want to say anything?" Betty shook her head. "How do I say goodbye? I can't say goodbye to my Eric, I can't. He can't be gone, he just can't, I have faith that he is still there, he can come back to us, he can." Bob walked back over to Betty and held her. She crumbled in his arms. It took every ounce of me to not burst into tears. I couldn't help it though, and a single tear rolled down my cheek as Bob turned back towards me. He walked over to me and gently wiped the tear from my cheek. I put my hand on top of his. "I'm so sorry there wasn't more we could do for your son." He smiled for the first time since I met him and said softly, "It's time."

    Together we walked back over to Eric's bedside. I pointed to the switch for the respirator. Bob reached out his hand—it was shaking slightly—and he turned the switch off. The respirator stopped moving up and down. As gently as I could I removed the tube that had been inserted into Eric's throat. Next, I turned off the heart monitor and together we removed all the sensors on Eric's body. Once we were done, the room was filled with silence. I wasn't prepared for that. I didn't tell them that this was the first time I had done this. They didn't tell you about the silence in the textbook. It was like someone was watching a TV show and they hit mute. None of us moved. We all, without noticing, held our breaths. The silence felt like an eternity. I knew it could take anywhere from a minute to ten minutes for Eric to pass, all the while his chest would move up and down giving his family the false hope that he was going to be able to breathe on his own. Bob sat down next to Betty and they just held each other. Bob's expression was blank while Betty looked hopefully at Eric, you could almost hear the prayers that she was thinking.

    I checked Eric's pulse and it had slowed noticeably since we turned the machines off. It wouldn't be long now...

# 11

# JACK

I left the Human Resources vault as quickly as I could. My plan was also running out of time; Ainsley and Brigida would return soon and Eric Frasier would be crossing over shortly. I closed the door and returned the keys to the drawer in Ainsley's desk. How much longer did I have before this crazy plan came crumbling down around me? I peeked my head out the door and at the end of the corridor Ainsley and Brigida were marching in my direction. They were clearly not too pleased. I shut the door as quickly as I could, hoping they hadn't seen me. I only had moments before I was caught. It was now or never. I closed my eyes and focused everything on Jess. I knew if I went back to her I would at least be in the same city as Eric Frasier. I didn't take the file with me in case that sent off some red flags with the powers that be. I knew Ainsley and Brigida had most likely figured out I wasn't meant to be there, but I was hoping that by not removing the file on Eric Frasier, I could hope to at least keep my motives a secret. But, if everything is already destined to happen, maybe this was all pointless and they knew exactly what I was going to do. But I had to at least try. I had all the information I needed, I knew where Eric Frasier was, and I knew I only had a few minutes left based off the information in his file. When I materialized at

New York General I had even less time. I moved as quickly as I could up to the ICU in search of his room. Once I arrived in the ICU wing another sensation hit me like a freight train.

Jess was here. I was excited and scared at the same time. Excited that if this worked I could find her right away. But on the other hand, I was scared. What would she think of me if she ever found out the truth about what I did, that I "borrowed" someone's body? I hadn't really thought about it until that moment. Eric Frasier had a family. Was he a father, did he have a wife, a girlfriend? I had to push those thoughts out of my head because there wasn't time to think about that. I needed to get back to Jess, I needed her to know I was all right. I needed her to be all right. I needed to be able to touch her one last time. But mostly, I needed her to know it was time to let me go and it was okay to do so. This was the only way I could do that. I ran into the room where Eric Frasier was set to pass in a little over a minute. There was no time for any more decisions, no second guessing, no worrying about the consequences.

I turned the corner into his room and froze in my tracks. I was looking at Jess. I had felt her in the hospital, but I hadn't realized she was going to be this close to what I was about to do. What sort of sick twist of fate was this, that of all the doctors in all the world, this man's doctor was my Jess. I looked around the room and seated nearby were two older people holding each other.

They must be his parents. Jess stood near Eric, and I could tell she had been trying to not cry. My Jess was still in there. She wasn't completely numb. Could I really go through with this? It is one thing to have a hypothetical plan because when it is not real, when it is not actualized, circumstances and consequences don't carry their true weight. But now that I was here and it was happening, the reality and the gravity of the situation was right there in front of me and couldn't be denied. I looked at the clock; only thirty seconds left. I had to make a decision. I was completely torn. On the one hand, I needed to help Jess move on with her life, I needed her to be the Jess she once was. I may never have this chance again. On the other hand, how could I destroy this family? How could

I make them think their son was still here? I looked back at the clock; only ten seconds left. I looked over at Eric's body and I saw the most amazing light begin to appear above his body. It was happening now, there was no more time to think. It was indescribable. It felt warm and inviting, like the feeling you get when you wrap yourself in your favorite blanket. The juxtaposition was not lost on me either, seeing the beauty that was beyond description while the people in the room were crying inconsolably. If only they could see what I was seeing, maybe it would make the transition easier. I counted the seconds down in my head.

9...8...7...6...5...

The light above his body continued to grow. It was nearly blinding. Looks like Eric was a good person, he was definitely on the way "up". That thought made me feel even worse than I already did; not only was I breaking Heaven's rules, I was doing it at the expense of an innocent soul. If Eric had been a shitty person I wouldn't be wavering as much as I was.

4...3...

I reacted before I could even think anymore. I got as close to Eric's body as I could. I wasn't sure exactly what

I was doing but I had to time it perfectly. I had to do it the second his soul left his body.

2...1...

I did the only thing I could think of and leaped into the air into the now-fading light above Eric's body...

# 12

## JESS

It had been close to ten minutes now since we turned off the machines. I took a step closer to his body and took Eric's arm and checked his pulse. Nothing. I unhooked my stethoscope and checked for a heartbeat. Nothing. I looked back towards Betty and Bob. "It's over, he's gone." The words had barely finished coming out of my mouth when Eric sat up and started coughing, trying to catch his breath! I screamed and jumped back across the room. Betty matched my scream, but hers was excitement. She jumped up and ran to her son's side. How the hell could this be happening? Eric should be dead. He had been brain dead for close to a week now. I had done everything right. I had followed the protocols. How was he now sitting upright and alive?

My head was spinning. I couldn't even begin to grasp what was happening, I made a huge mistake. I went through it all again in my head. I tried to form words, a thought, anything to say to Betty and Bob but I just couldn't. It shouldn't be happening. It went against everything I had learned. I had no explanation for what I was seeing. Betty was crying tears of joy now and hugging Eric who was still
   coughing and trying to catch his breath. I ran over to him and started checking his vitals and sure enough he now had a pulse. I was in shock.

There was no medical explanation for this. I can't even begin to describe what I was feeling. Eric was alive and that was amazing news. But, I had also failed this family. I had failed Betty and Bob, two people I had come to care about despite my best efforts. I had told them there was nothing that could save their son. He was gone. But I was wrong. He was alive and I had failed him too. I pulled out my penlight and shone it in his eyes and they had the appropriate pupillary response. Everything was checking out. How had this all changed from one second to the next? I looked him in the eyes. "Eric, Eric, my name is Dr. Miller, do you know where you are?" There was no response, he just continued to cough. He couldn't seem to catch his breath. I grabbed the oxygen mask and placed it over his mouth as best I could. "Eric, Eric, I need you to look at me, try to take a deep breath, in through your nose and out through your mouth." His eyes met mine, and for a brief second, I had this really strong sense that I knew him. Something in his eyes looked familiar, but then it was gone. Eric was slowly starting to calm down with the help of the oxygen mask. My

first priority was to make sure he was stable, make sure everything was okay, but then I was going to get to the bottom of this. For whatever reason their son was still here. I didn't want to think of the word because I am a doctor and doctors don't believe in miracles, we believe in science and what can be proved, but this was a miracle if there ever was one. Once Betty had calmed down a little, she came over to me and put her arms around me and held me close. When she let go of me, she walked back over to Eric and put her arms around him. "I knew you would come back to us, I prayed and prayed, and God listened."

# 13

# BETTY

When I was a little girl, I would spend hours and hours in my room playing with my dolls. I was an only child, so in a way, they were like my brothers and sisters, but they were also my children and I took care of them as if they were family. Oh, how I loved those dolls! They were more than just toys to me. I knew from a young age I wanted to have babies of my own one day. I didn't know then how hard that would be.

I met Bob shortly after I finished high school. It was love at first sight. I was working at my parent's diner.

I'd worked there since I was a teenager. I know I should have hated it; teenagers usually hate everything their parents make them do, but I loved it. Everyone in our small little town knew who I was, and they all got to watch me grow up. My favorites were Sunday morning when everyone would come to the diner after church. I remember how I loved to see everyone coming into the restaurant all dressed up. My first job at the diner was hostess, but eventually as I got older, my parents moved me up to

waitress. My mom was so proud of me. She would always tell me how much I reminded her of herself.

I met Bob one night after a football game. I couldn't go to the game because I had to work. That was the only downside of the diner; I didn't really get to be a kid and go to things like football games and dances. But I honestly didn't mind that much. My parents had instilled in me a strong work ethic, so I never really saw being busy as a negative, it's just what we had to do as a family to make ends meet. Plus, my parents were happy to let me spend my tips on anything I wanted because I had worked hard and earned it. Bob had moved to our town during our senior year and joined the football team. He was in the popular clique in a matter of days. I wasn't popular and I wasn't unpopular, I was just Betty who worked at the diner.

Meeting Bob that day in the diner changed my life. He came in with his friends to celebrate another win and I walked over to take their order. We'd crossed paths once or twice, but I was pretty sure he didn't know I existed. The moment he looked me in the eyes, I knew nothing would ever be the same. There was a kindness in his eyes that reminded me of my father.

They say girls always marry their fathers, and, in this case, they were right. My dad was the kindest man I had ever known and whenever he looked at my mother you could see his heart melting, even after 30 years of marriage. I wanted to find that for myself. And the good Lord blessed me, because I did find that, with Bob. After he had dinner with his friends, he stayed behind to talk to me. I couldn't talk much because we still had a full diner from the football game. He sat there quietly for hours drinking milkshakes at the counter. My parents could see there was something between us. Bob even helped me clean up after the diner closed. Once everything was finished, he asked my parents for permission to walk me home. Times were different back then. Men were gentlemen. My parents agreed and we set off.

My heart was beating so fast the entire time. We would go long stretches without saying a word to each other. But it was never awkward. About halfway to my house he reached out and took my hand in his and

I could have just died. I couldn't hide the smile on my face, and neither could he.

We just fit together. And that moment right there was when I knew I would marry him one day and he would be the father of my children. Getting married was the easy part, but our journey to become parents was a long and painful one.

Bob asked me to marry him shortly after my twentieth birthday, which back then, was a bit late. Most of my girlfriends were already either engaged, married, or working on their first child. I didn't mind that I was behind, in comparison to my friends. I'd always been a pretty independent kind of girl and things with Bob just never seemed to be in a rush. I was over the moon when Bob proposed, and our wedding was perfect. We didn't have much money, but my parents let us get married in the backyard. Once we got married, we got a small place of our own and began trying to have a family. We were both on the same page; we wanted at least three or four kids and we wanted to be young parents, because we wanted to be young grandparents and hopefully one day be great-grandparents. We were both very traditional; family was everything to us. Our plans, it turned out, weren't very realistic. We tried for five years to have children and nothing happened. Each month that passed without getting pregnant, I became more and more despondent.

We went to every doctor we could find to see what the problem was. And all of them assured us of the same thing—

we were both perfectly healthy and there was nothing stopping us from getting pregnant. I'm a very upbeat person but those years took a toll on me. I felt like a failure as a woman. A failure as a wife. Bob couldn't have been more amazing. He was truly my rock through our entire ordeal. I don't think I would have been able to get through it with a lesser man than Bob Frasier. But even he couldn't keep my spirits up as the years dragged on. I had resigned myself to the fact that maybe I would never become a mother. Some nights I would cry myself to sleep thinking about the dolls I had all those years ago. Was that the closest I would ever get to motherhood? Bob suggested that perhaps we try adoption. At first, I didn't want to talk about it because I wanted to have children of my own. I wanted to experience giving birth. But over the years I started to warm up to the idea of adoption. If it was the only way for us to be parents, then we would embrace it and welcome a child into our lives who needed a loving home.

The other thing that happened during those years was that I found my way back to God. My parents had always been fairly religious. They raised me in the Catholic faith but at a certain age they allowed me to make my own decisions as far as what I did and did not believe. I had always believed in God; there was too much beauty and wonder in the world for someone to not have had a divine hand in creating it. I just didn't necessarily believe that if you prayed to God he would answer your prayers. But dealing with my infertility issues was more than I could handle. My mother suggested that maybe I needed to go back to church, find my faith again, and pray to God for help. At first, I thought it was a ridiculous idea, but truthfully, that was my anger talking. I was angry that the thing I wanted most in the world seemed to be just outside of my grasp. But I did listen to my mother and I started going back to church regularly. I went to confession, I lit candles and prayed to God that he would find in his divine wisdom that Bob and I were worthy of being parents.

Nothing changed for months. But the strangest thing began to happen. The more I went to church and spoke with God, the more at peace I was that this was the path God had set out in front of us. For the first time in five years I was at peace with the fact that I may never have a child of my own.

It was the summer of 1983 when Bob and I decided it was time to pursue adoption. And that is when it happened, our little miracle. Bob had taken me out to dinner at our

favorite steakhouse and, about fifteen minutes into our meal, I was hit with a wave of dizziness. I tried to get up to go to the bathroom and I ended up passing out right there in the middle of the restaurant. Can you believe it? How embarrassing!

Once I came to, Bob insisted we go to the hospital immediately to make sure I was okay. And that is when we found out I was pregnant. All my prayers had come true, I was going to be a mom. That cemented my faith in God. I had prayed for a miracle and God gave me one, my Eric. I know every parent says their child is a little Angel, even when it's obvious they are a brat. But that wasn't the case with Eric. He was the sweetest little boy. We kept trying to have more children after that, but I was never able to get pregnant again. It didn't matter because we had Eric, our miracle.

When Eric moved away to go to college it broke my heart but that is something that all parents must go through, letting their little ones leave the nest. It's true that you will always see your children as just that, children, no matter how big they are. After college Eric decided he wanted to live in New York. I was worried about the big city corrupting him, but I soon realized it was an

unnecessary worry. We didn't get to see Eric as often as we wanted to but when we did he was the same sweet boy he had always been. I knew his job was stressful, and he was working such long hours but whenever we were in town, he always made time to be our tour guide. And when we couldn't come for a visit, he always made time to talk. He and I had a standing Sunday morning talk over coffee. I looked forward to those conversations all week. Bob and I felt very blessed, and then it all collapsed around us.

It was 3:12pm on a Tuesday when I got the call that Eric had been in a skiing accident. I didn't hear the rest of what the doctors told me. The only thing I could think about was that I had to get to New York to be with him.

When we arrived the sight of him stopped me in my tracks. There were so many machines, wires and tubes. My son looked so small in the bed. That is when I met Dr. Jess Miller, Eric's doctor. She tried to explain to me what happened, but I couldn't focus on anything other than Eric. He was in a coma and they weren't sure he was going to ever wake up. How could this be happening? How could he be taken away from me now? I didn't know what to do with myself. The only thing I could do was pray, so that is what I did. Every day I would go to the church near the hospital. I would pray to

God that he would protect and heal my Eric. You have to have faith. Faith that your prayers will be heard if you believe enough in the wisdom and virtue of God. And I did.

I believed with every fiber of my being that God would hear my prayers and save our son. I prayed every single morning for nearly a month. Dr. Miller was so kind and made time for us every day. They kept telling us Eric wasn't making any progress, but I believed in my heart that with God's help, Eric would come back to us. How could I have been so wrong? How could it have come to this? The doctors had decided Eric was brain dead and there was nothing more they could do for him. At first, I didn't hear anything they were saying. My mind was moving in slow motion. This couldn't be the end. Eric has to come back to us. Or was I wrong about all of this? Was I wrong about Eric being a miracle? Did God not hear my prayers all those years ago?

Bob tried to make me understand that this was for the best, for Eric. I didn't want to hear it. I just wanted my son to come back to me. Bob was always the stronger of the two of us. He had to do it. I couldn't turn my son's life off. I was numb inside, I was broken.

When Bob turned off the last machine, it was the worst moment of my life. My son was dead. I wanted to go with him. What was the point of living in a world without Eric? I was hopeless. But then, in an instant, my hope was restored. My faith was rewarded. My life was saved when Eric sat up. God had heard my prayers. God saved my miracle. God is good!

## 14

## JACK

Did it work? The last thing I remembered was seeing the light as Eric's soul began to leave his body. Had I swapped places with him? My vision was cloudy. As things started to clear up, I realized it had worked. I was sitting up in the hospital bed where Eric was. I could feel...I could feel! The sheets felt soft on my legs. My eyes burned as they tried to adjust to the light in the room. I had that familiar tickle in my throat that makes you cough when you have a cold or when you drink water and it goes down the wrong pipe. I can't explain how good it felt to feel again. I wanted to savor every moment because I didn't know how long it was going to last. For all I knew, as quickly as I entered Eric's body I would be expelled. I wanted to get up and run down the hallway, eat a doughnut, drink a cup of coffee. My mind was racing with limitless possibilities. All I could think about were all the things I had missed that I would get to enjoy again. And then there was Jess. But then Eric's mother rushed over and hugged me and all of those hopes and thoughts crashed down around me.

What have I done? That was all I could think as this woman was embracing who she thought was her son. How could I tell this woman her son was in fact gone, that I was just a temporary 'passenger' in his body, if that's even what I was? I wasn't even sure I would be able to stay for long.

What if I was gone in a matter of moments and she had to feel the devastation of losing him all over again? I wanted to pull away from her and talk to Jess while there was still time. But I couldn't bring myself to do it. This poor family has already been through so much and here they thought a miracle had happened and they had their son back. I didn't think it through. I just...I can't take away this family's joy. I just can't. What I had done was unthinkable, I was just so consumed with Jess that I didn't fully consider the ramifications of my actions. I needed to make it right, but it might be too late for that. But there is something that I can do, something I can do for Eric's family. I decided in that moment I would keep my secret from them and from Jess, for now. I would let them believe I was indeed Eric Frasier who miraculously came back to them. I would wait till the time was right and I was alone with Jess before I told her the truth. But what if she didn't believe me?

And how would I pretend to be this man I knew nothing about? I couldn't fake something like that; his family would know something wasn't right. They wouldn't have a clue what was actually going on, that I was wearing Eric like a winter coat, but they would be able to sense something was off. I thought about what I could do and the only thing that came to mind was saying I didn't remember. It sounds cliché, but amnesia seemed like the best idea at the time. It wouldn't be too out of the realm of possibility that someone who had been through a traumatic injury like Eric had might have some residual memory loss.

Jess walked over to me. "Do you know where you are, Eric?" I wanted to shout, "I'm not Eric, I'm Jack! Jess, it's me! I came back for you!" But I couldn't. I looked up and lied to Jess for the first time since I met her all those years ago, "No, where am I?" It was a surreal feeling to speak and not hear your own voice. Eric's voice was deeper than mine and had a hint of a Midwestern accent.

Jess took my hands and I shuddered. "My name is Dr. Miller, Eric, you are at New York General Hospital. You were in a skiing accident, what is the last thing you remember?" Well, I didn't remember anything; I wasn't Eric. This was already spiraling out of control, but I had no choice but

to keep going. "The last thing I remember is being on the mountain." Eric's mother looked at me nervously then over at Jess. "Is that normal, Dr. Miller, for Eric to not remember anything?" Jess shook her head. "To be honest, Betty, we are completely out of the realm of what's normal. Based on all I know and every test I ran, your son was clinically deceased and now, now he's not. So, we just have to be patient." Jess looked over at Eric's father. "How are you holding up, Bob?" Bob had been sitting there staring at the floor for the last few minutes. He looked up at Jess. "I'm not sure, Dr. Miller. Am I grateful? Yes, but are we sure this isn't temporary, has this ever happened before?" Over the next hour or so Jess explained to Betty and Bob that just to be safe they were going to run a series of tests on Eric, on me, to see exactly what was going on and then they would have a better idea of whether this was a temporary state or if their son had come back from the dead. Every time Jess said something like that my heart sunk just a little bit more. I don't know how long I am going to be able to keep up this charade.

Jess had me lie down on the table as she checked my heart and started jotting down notes in her chart. Then she took a few vials of blood for testing. Once that was all

done, I was wheeled out of the room and sent to radiology where they did a series of X-rays, CAT scans, EEGs, and a dozen other tests I had never seen or heard of. I was exhausted and before I knew it, I had fallen asleep. When I came to several hours had passed and Betty and Bob were nowhere to be found, thankfully. I slowly sat up and Jess was sitting in the chair across from me. I asked where they were, and Jess told me she sent them home to get some rest. Finally, we were alone. She walked over and pulled a chair close to my bed. I could smell her perfume. She still wore the same perfume I used to buy her. It made me smile. Jess smiled back. "Well, it looks like someone is feeling better. How are you, Eric?" For a second, only a second, I forgot I wasn't me—to Jess, I was Eric. I needed more time to think about what I was going to say to her so I decided to just play along for now. "Well, I was dead this morning and now I'm not so I can't complain." Jess laughed; God, I'd missed that laugh. "So what did all those tests say, am I a zombie?" Jess opened the chart she was holding. "Quite the opposite. We ran every test in the book, and everything came back normal. There is no more swelling in your brain, nothing. As far as I can tell, you are a perfectly healthy young man." I took her hand. She touched my shoulder and I felt a tingle shoot up my arm. You'll never understand how much you miss being able to touch someone, something, anything, until you can't anymore. I lost my train of thought for a second but regained myself "Does that mean I can go home soon?" She smiled back at me. "We are going to keep you overnight for observation. Besides, do you even know where home is?" She was right. I had no idea where Eric lived. Hopefully Betty and Bob would be able to help with that. I took her hand. "Can I ask you something?" She nodded and I tried my best to smile. "What would you say if I asked you out to dinner?" She pulled her hand back and stood up. Her smile faded and she looked at me seriously. "I would say no, I'm your doctor and you are my patient, it wouldn't be appropriate." I sat up in bed as she moved closer to the door. "Well, as soon as I get out of here tomorrow, you technically won't be my doctor anymore, will you? So, I'll ask you again tomorrow and we can take it from there. Deal?" She tried to hold back a smile. "We'll see, get some rest, Eric." I nodded and smiled. "Will do.

Goodnight, Jess." Jess's smile disappeared. Shit! Eric didn't know her name, but I did. I tried to cover my tracks as best I could. "My mom told me your name while you were out of the room." She nodded her head approvingly.

"Goodnight, Eric." And with that, she walked out of the room. I rolled over and tried to get some rest. As I drifted off, I could have sworn I saw the outline of Alistair's red coat. But I was too tired to open my eyes again.

## 15

## ALISTAIR

I have been a Guardian Angel for so long that it's often difficult now to remember my human life with any degree of certainty. I was born on the coast of England in a small town called Brighton in the year of our Lord, 1771. Brighton today is a thriving seaside metropolis. However, when I was alive it was a different story. Brighton was originally a busy fishing town but most of the city and the port were destroyed in the early 1700s. Eventually the town had a resurgence in the mid-1750s, which is when my family decided to move from the crowded and generally unsafe life they had been living in East London, in an area called Whitechapel. That neighborhood would become famous, or infamous, in the late 19th century as it was the hunting ground of one Jack the Ripper. My parents decided London was no place to raise a family, so they took every cent they had and left for the coast, hoping for a better life. Shortly after they had made the journey to Brighton my mother discovered she was with child, again. My parents were overjoyed and by the end of that year I was born.

Their joy was short lived as my mother died in childbirth in the summer of 1774. The midwife was only able to save my baby sister Juliana. I was only a child at the time but even I could see my father was a changed man. The light in his eyes had gone. He no longer took care of us and I suspected as I got older that he never loved Juliana because she had taken his love away from him. He blamed her for his unfortunate circumstances. My father sunk into deep melancholia and turned to drink to numb his pain. With my father consumed with other endeavors I was left to raise my dear Juliana. As such we were virtually inseparable. Up until my death she would always tell me that she loved me not like a brother but like a father. Our family's financial standing continued to deteriorate as a result of my father's waywardness. I had never married because Juliana would be left to fend for herself. In those days, women had no rights until they were married off. Until that day came, I was her protector. I planned to stay with the family until Juliana was safely married and since we had no dowry to speak of, it was a difficult prospect. In order to save for a modest dowry, I was forced to volunteer for the militia in the winter of 1795, just short of my twenty-fourth birthday. Without my help, Juliana was destined for a spinster's life. Her happiness and safety were of

paramount concern to me. At the time, Britain had been at war with France for 3 years as Napoleon Bonaparte and his allies had been expanding their empire in an ever-growing campaign to control Europe. Once I completed training, I was sent to join the war. Military life was difficult, and I knew once I left Britain the likelihood that I would return unharmed was slim at best. There was a greater chance than naught that I would never return. Juliana was heartbroken when I left but the decision had been made. She would write me letters as often as she could. She would talk about how things were changing in Brighton as new roads and houses were being built. Those letters were the only comforts I was afforded.

I remained in the military for the next six years.

Over time I had risen in the ranks to a general, through a combination of determination and the deaths of fellow soldiers, creating a need for others to command battalions. I had managed to save enough money to provide my sister with a dowry for marriage and I was looking forward to coming home to Brighton and resuming my life with her when I died. I had been fighting in Egypt when it happened. My battalion was ambushed by French forces and I, along with several other soldiers, were killed by cannon fire. It

happened so fast that there was no pain. I was grateful for that because of my relationship with Juliana I was allowed to return to Earth and watch over her, as her Guardian Angel. I remained by her side until her death. Juliana never married and died of cholera in 1822. Her death brought the end of our familial bloodline. Juliana crossed over. After her soul departed, I was assigned charges depending on the need and decisions that came down from the Council of Angels. The Council is how I came to watch over Jack Richardson. Over the years as I watched over him, I came to realize he was a good person with a genuine heart, and I enjoyed seeing him fall for Jess Miller. I was not made aware of his destiny until the day he crossed over.

The only entities that are aware of the fate of humans are the select few that work for the office of Human Resources, the Council of Angels, and God himself. For Guardian Angels, it is easier that way.

In Heaven, as on Earth, there are structures in place to preserve order. The Council of Angels is one such body. The Council is comprised not of Guardian Angels—humans that had crossed over—but Grigori, the eighth Choir of Angels.

The Grigori, also known as the Watchers, were created by God to be the first Shepherds of Humanity. The Council oversaw all connections between the Earthly plane and Heaven. It was a monumental daily task but the Grigori, and all Angels for that matter, were created to serve God and his will.

The Grigori have a somewhat sullied reputation. They were created to watch over Humanity but their time on Earth affected them. They began to lust after those they were created to watch over, which resulted in a race of beings known as the Nephilim, half-human, half-Angel. Those who choose to disobey God remain fallen for all eternity. The rest of the Grigori make up the Council of Angels.

I was not aware of Jack's actions until it was too late. His choice to circumvent the laws of Heaven had far greater consequences than I could have possibly imagined. It was that singular decision that changed the course of all our lives...that changed Heaven itself. I was summoned before the Council of Angels. The Council ensures that both realms abide by the rules decreed by God. This is not the word of God as written in the Human Bible. Much of the Bible is flawed as it is written by man, not by God. As I entered the room I was greeted by the seven members of the Council. One is not called to appear for pleasantries. The Council not only ensures that God's law is followed, they also enforce the punishments when those rules and laws are broken.

The Grigori are rather imposing. Envision a man roughly nine to ten feet tall and silent. Their silence was another feature that distinguished them from humans.

Grigori never spoke, rather, they communicated through a form of telepathy. Angels are not limited by the constructs that define humanity.

Within moments of entering the room the sheer weight of what Jack had done was laid out plainly before me. How could he have been so blind, so naïve to think he could outsmart the Creator? The utter hubris of humanity, of this human in particular. I attempted to ask why he was not prevented from achieving his goal, but before I could even begin my sentence, they had already answered it. The thoughts appeared in my head in rapid succession. The summation of their argument was that humanity had Free Will. God had granted man the ability to choose their own fate. Jack had chosen to defy God. He would have to also choose to return and suffer the consequences of his indiscretions. There was nothing I could do to force him to return but I would plead with him to listen to reason. I would implore him to make things right. And given what I

was told about what was about to happen I knew time was short. I had to return to Earth and find Jack. But where was I to begin? I could no longer feel my connection to him. Everything depended on what would happen in the next few days. I left Heaven lost and confused. I hadn't felt like that in over two hundred years.

# 16

# JACK

Waking up this morning I had almost forgotten everything that had happened in the last few days. I got up and walked into the bathroom and it wasn't until I looked in the mirror and didn't see myself looking back that it all came flooding back to me. I was no longer me. As far as the world knew I was Eric Frasier. I know I couldn't keep this going for long and I know what I was doing to Betty and Bob was unimaginable, but I selfishly put those feelings aside because all I could think about was Jess.

Figuring out how to make things right would have to come later. And since they had done every test under the sun and found nothing technically wrong with me, they were releasing me—releasing Eric—from the hospital.

I did not want to leave the hospital because leaving the hospital meant leaving Jess, and Jess was the only reason for what I had done. But what choice did I have? How strange would it look for me to say I didn't want to leave?

I had no belongings so when Betty and Bob arrived, I was ready to go. Jess accompanied them as they walked into the room and all I wanted to do was scream, "I'm not Eric,

I'm Jack! Jess, it's me!" But I didn't. How do you casually tell someone that? "Oh hey I'm not really what you see, I'm not really Eric, I'm actually your dead fiancé walking around in an Eric Frasier suit." How do you say that without sounding completely insane? So, I didn't say anything. I gave her a hug, said thank you for taking care of me, and left with Betty and Bob.

Riding home from the hospital in the back of Betty and Bob's rental car went by in a blur. I barely said a word; what was there to say? They didn't know it, but they were complete strangers to me. I just stared blankly out the window as if I were seeing New York for the first time, and in a way, I was. These were not my eyes, it all felt surreal and strange, foreign almost. As much as I had hoped to come back, now that I actually was it was like I was experiencing everything for the first time. We passed by blocks I had known quite well but they didn't have the sense of familiarity I expected them to have. I wondered if there were any residual parts of Eric still here. Could that explain why I felt the way I did? Soon enough I would find out just how wrong that thought was. Betty snapped me out of my daze. "Eric, honey, does anything look familiar to you?" I told her no and she reached behind her and

gently rubbed my knee and said, "Don't worry, honey, in time it will all come back to you, I have faith." I wanted to tell her the truth then and there and be done with it, maybe they would understand what I had done. But who was I kidding, of course they wouldn't understand, so I kept my mouth shut.

Eventually we pulled up outside a building in the Meatpacking District. Back when Jess and I first moved to New York this area was still up and coming, but my time away had definitely changed things. It looked like a really nice neighborhood now as I saw trendy-looking people walking down the street and a young woman taking her dog for a walk. Bob turned off the car and all three of us exited. I looked around it was a nice street with some trees lining both sides. As we closer to the building the doorman greeted me, "Good morning, Mr. Frasier, nice to see you again." At first, I didn't respond I just looked at him and nodded. Betty took my hand and thanked the doorman as he held the door open for us. The elevator came to a stop on the seventh floor and I snapped out of my fog. I let Eric's parents out first since I didn't know which direction I was going. Betty made a left out of the elevator and Bob and I followed. Betty stopped at apartment

7D, fished out a set of keys from her pocket and looked towards me. "Would you like to do the honors, Eric?" I smiled politely and told her no. Betty gave me that motherly smile, a mixture of happiness and worry. She was clearly happy to have her son back, but also worried I wasn't quite myself. She was right of course. Betty turned back towards the door and opened it and we walked inside.

I stood in the doorway taking in the room. Eric's apartment was definitely a bachelor pad. In the center was a black leather couch and a couple of recliners facing a big mounted TV on the farthest wall. In a weird way, I felt slightly relieved because it was clear Eric did not have a girlfriend, at least not one he lived with anyway. There wasn't a woman's touch in the place, save for a set of fresh flowers sitting on the coffee table. Immediately I knew those were from Betty. She saw me eyeing the calla lilies and smiled. "Do you like them, Eric? I thought it'd help to brighten up the place a bit and welcome you home." Flowers were never really my thing but I didn't know if Eric liked flowers or not so I just smiled and said thank you. Next, Betty walked over to the kitchen and I followed, passing a mountain bike and some extra skiing equipment that was resting near the closet. Apparently, Eric was the

outdoorsy type. Betty opened the fridge and started talking about all the things she had picked up. It was then that I got a glimpse of her nerves; her hands shook slightly as she rummaged through the fridge.

I wondered what she was thinking. Was she noticing things that were different about her son? Was she worried that having her son back was just temporary? I could only imagine the parade of thoughts that must've been going through her head. Yesterday she said goodbye to her son and today here he was, her only child, in his apartment, alive. We were all in uncharted territory, even if it was for different reasons. I told them that I was tired and wanted to get some rest. After the words came out of my mouth, Betty looked over at me and I saw her heart sink, just for a second, but she recovered and replaced that look of concern with her warm smile, covering up all of her internal emotions. She took her husband's hand and he gave her a gentle kiss on the cheek. Their connection was obvious. I'd always thought Jess and I would be like that when we were old, still as in love as the day we met. Betty shut the fridge and walked over towards me, putting on a brave face. "You get some rest, honey. Let us know if you need anything, we are staying at the Hilton. I left the number on the fridge so it would be easy to find." She kissed me on the cheek. "Thanks B—" I redirected my words. "Thanks, Mom." And with that they left and closed the door behind them. I looked around the apartment and had an overwhelming feeling I was intruding. I was an intruder in Eric's apartment, his life, even his body. The longer I lived inside him, the more guilt I felt.

I walked around looking at all the knick-knacks and the pictures on the wall. One photo was of Eric and his friends laughing in what looked like a ski lodge. Another photo was a group of people and Eric celebrating at a New Year's Eve party. The final photo was a family photo of Bob and Betty and what looked to be a ten-year-old Eric and a large golden retriever sitting on the front porch smiling. Was that their house? They looked like the quintessential American family. And as I stared at his life in 5x7 glossies, I was hit with a wave of sadness. Eric had an entire life. A life that was now over, even if no one in that life knew about it. The sadness was followed by a wave of exhaustion that hit me hard. I couldn't remember the last time I was that tired. I barely made it to the bed before I was unconscious, still wearing the clothes Betty and Bob had brought to the hospital for me.

I woke up the next morning and I still felt tired but not nearly as much as the night before. I made my way into the kitchen and opened the fridge to see what Betty had brought for me to eat. It all looked way too healthy for my tastes. Back when I was alive, Jess used to make fun of me because I basically ate like a five-year-old. For breakfast, I would usually have cereal, and not the healthy kind, the kind that left you most excited for the sugary milk that remained when you were finished eating the cereal part. I dug around a little more past all the vegetables and bottles of juice and water and managed to find a big chocolate bar. Well done, Betty! I unwrapped it and took a big bite—god, I had forgotten how good chocolate tastes.

Then I made a big cup of coffee and sat at the table to figure out what I was going to do with my first real day back on Earth.

First up, I gave Betty a call to let her know I was okay and to make dinner plans. After that, the only thing I could think of was Jess. She was the reason I came back and since I didn't know how long I had here, I had to figure out what I was going to do. After I finished eating and downing some caffeine, which weirdly didn't have the usual wake-up effect that it had in the past, I had a quick shower and then headed out to see if Jess had changed her mind about spending some time with Eric. I left the apartment and retraced my steps to get back to the hospital. I turned the last corner and the hospital came into view. It was then that I realized I hadn't really planned out what I was going to say to Jess. She had already turned me down once, what if she did it again? What if all this was in vain? I was deep in thought when I heard someone call for Eric. I turned around and there she was—my Jess. I couldn't contain my smile. She walked up to me and I hoped to see my enthusiasm returned but to Jess I was simply her patient. She looked me up and down. "Is everything okay, Eric? You aren't due for a follow-up for a few days." My smile faded slightly, but there was no turning back now. I had decided I would act as though it was my last day on Earth, and for all that I knew it could be, so it was time for a charm offensive. I looked at her and tried to give her my most charming smile, hoping Eric's had the same effect on Jess that my smile did when I was alive. I watched her face for some sort of reaction.

Nothing! Ooookay, new tactic, I would have to use my words to get her to spend some time with me.

I cleared my throat and began, "Good morning, Jess." She interrupted me, "It's Dr. Miller, Eric." This was going to be harder than I thought. I took a deep breath and continued, "Well, seeing as you saved my life, I think it's only fair that I get to call you something other than Dr. Miller...and I was hoping to revisit our conversation from the other day. Will you let me take you out?" I followed that up with a pretty good set of puppy eyes if I do say so myself. And then I saw it, a little chink in the armor Jess had put up. She hesitated briefly. "Eric, while I'm flattered, it would be unethical for me to see you, I am your doctor." Now it was my turn to interrupt her. "Well, seeing as you discharged me yesterday you technically aren't my doctor anymore, right? I mean, my follow-up appointments are with Dr. Anderson so I don't see anything wrong with you letting me take you out." Jess tried to object but I pressed on, "If I've learned anything it's that life is short and if you want something you should go after it. For all I know, today could be my last day on Earth." It was a cheap shot that I knew would get to Jess, considering the things I had heard her say at my funeral, but it was true and it was worth the risk. I stared at Jess waiting for some sign of what she was thinking, but I

didn't know this Jess. I wasn't sure how she was going to react, but I felt like I was starting to get through to her so I pressed on further. I tried to lighten my tone so it sounded more playful and less pushy. "Just come for a walk with me in the park, grab a coffee or something,"

I offered, casually reaching out and taking her hand.

At first, she tried to pull away, but I held firm. She looked up at me and our eyes met, and just for a moment I felt like she saw me, the real me, and not just Eric. She took a quick breath in and broke eye contact with me, looking down at the ground. "Okay, but just a coffee. When do you want to go?" I couldn't contain my smile. "No time like the present," I told her. She shook her head. "I can't go now, I have to go to work." It took a little more convincing but I was finally able to get her to take a personal day. As she was talking to her boss I continued to smirk and give her two thumbs up. She almost started laughing and gently pushed me. I was struck with a strong sense of déjà vu. Jess used to do the same thing to me when I was acting like a goofball while she was trying to be serious. My Jess was still in there, she was just buried under years of loneliness, but she was there. After she hung up the phone we turned and starting walking towards

the park. She looked at me and sincerely asked, "How do I know you aren't some kind of stalker or a crazy person? I mean, I know nothing about you." If she only knew how wrong she was there, but I responded, "I promise I'm not a crazy person, but I did die yesterday so I can't promise that I'm not a zombie. I have had some pretty weird cravings this morning!" I growled and pretended to bite her neck. She squealed, laughed, and skipped ahead of me. I dragged one leg behind me and put on my best zombie voice. "Jess, Jess wait for me, I'm sooo hungry!" She was genuinely laughing for I think the first time in longer than she would probably admit. The revelation hit her too because she instantly stopped and just stared at me. I dropped the zombie act, walked up to her, and extended my hand. She looked at me so intently as if she were looking right through me and I could almost hear her heart beating, beating like it was going to burst out of her chest.

Without saying a word she slid her hand into mine and we walked off towards the park in silence.

We walked for a few minutes, hand in hand. Near the fountain I got us a couple of coffees and a few little pastries to nibble on and we found a spot to sit down. It reminded me of one of our first dates back in high school.

I had no money, so I picked up some doughnuts and a couple of sodas and we sat in the park and just talked for hours.

It's funny, I got so lost in that moment I almost entirely forgot about my plan. In a strange way, it felt like I was given a gift and I got to relive our first date. Once we finally sat down Jess let go of my hand, but her eyes were still on me. She looked down at her coffee, smiled slightly and took a little sip. "Is everything okay?" I asked her. She looked back up at me, but this time there was a sadness in her eyes, the same look I had seen on her when she was watching old home movies alone in her apartment. She breathed in deeply through her mouth and slowly exhaled through her nose before saying, "It's just that you remind me of someone I used to know a long time ago."

I nodded, fairly certain I knew where the conversation was going, but I tried my best to only ask questions someone who knew nothing would ask. I took a sip of my coffee. "So who do I remind you of?" She asked me why I wanted to know, and I replied, "Just curious, I guess." She took her time thinking about it, whether or not to open up to this complete stranger about something so personal. It must have been a real struggle because we sat there for

several minutes, the only sounds between us the occasional sip of coffee or the rustling pastry bags. Finally, she started, "His name was Jack and he was my fiancé. He passed away a long time ago." She turned her gaze from me and looked off into the distance. An eternity passed between us. I was about to speak but Jess beat me to it, starting to get up. "I'm sorry, Eric, but I can't do this." I could see that I was getting nowhere and, honestly, I was starting to feel like I was lying to her. I lying to her. I reached out and took her hand, trying to calm the situation. "Jess, don't go, stay, please. How about you tell me about Jack?" Talk about surreal. I thought it was weird hearing people talk about me at my funeral; that didn't hold a candle to asking the love of your life to tell you about YOU. Jess hesitated for a minute and then sat back down and pulled her hand back from mine. "I'm sorry, it's just been a really long time since I've done anything like this." I wanted to take the pressure off her so I figured it would be easier for me to just ask her questions about me. I didn't want to ask her about what happened to me, that was a painful enough memory for the both of us, so I wanted to try and keep things light. I asked, "What is it about me that reminds you of Jack?" She

smirked slightly. "I don't know, it's something in your eyes, I mean they aren't even the same color, Jack had brown eyes, but there is a kindness in your eyes that reminds me of him, I guess. Is this weird, talking about him?" I took a bite of my muffin and replied, "Not at all, we are getting to know each other, and he has obviously had an important effect on your life. What was he like, if you don't mind me asking?" She looked at me with this combination of gratitude and relief. "Well, first of all, he was a total pain in the ass!" I burst out laughing, it wasn't what I was expecting her to say, and in her defense, I could definitely be a pain in the ass sometimes...okay, most times. She took another sip of her coffee, her shoulders relaxed, and I felt like she was finally responding to me, to Eric. She continued, "But he was a

pain in the ass, you know? He could drive me up the wall sometimes, but then, other times, the way he would look at me or grab my hand randomly made me feel like we were the only two people in the world. Have you ever felt that?" I nodded slightly and told her, "Maybe." She continued, "He was my partner in crime, I guess that's the best way to describe it. We had a lot of things in common, we were both obsessed with Oscar Wilde—" And then I blurted out, before

I realized what I was saying, "I love Oscar Wilde!" She looked at me, surprised. "You do?" It was too late to backpedal so I tried to play it off. "Doesn't everyone?"

That was the best I could come up with, not the strongest comeback I realize but it seemed to sort of work. She asked me what my favorite Oscar Wilde novel was. I knew ours was The Importance of Being Earnest, but I said it was The Picture of Dorian Gray. Jess nodded. "That's a good one, but I'm more partial to his lighter work. Jack and I had always wanted to go to Paris to see his tomb, but we never made it." She trailed off slightly and seemed to get lost in her head. She regrouped and asked me, "Have you ever been?" I shook my head no. She was right though, we'd always wanted to go but there was always an excuse, we were busy, or we never had the money and then we ran out of time. I asked her if she still wanted to go someday and the sadness came flooding back into her eyes. She said, "I don't know, part of me does but I'm afraid it would be cheating on Jack. I know that sounds crazy, but it was OUR thing and I'm not sure how I would feel if I went without him. It might be too hard, or too sad, I don't know." I took her hands and looked deep into her eyes. "Well, if I were Jack, I would want you to go. Think of it as one final adventure." I needed to qualify the thought a bit, so I added, "I didn't know him, but I have a feeling anyone worthy of someone like you would want you to find happiness again. And the truth is people never leave us, not the ones who mean the most to us, they are always with us in here." I put my hand on my chest, just over my heart.

Jess started to laugh; she used to make fun of me for being a bit corny sometimes. It was like no time had passed. Jess, in between giggles, said, "That was really cheesy. You know that, right?" I grinned back at her. "Maybe a little." Our eyes locked again. We just stared at each other, drinking each other in. I whispered that I was going to kiss her. She just nodded slightly, parted her lips, and closed her eyes. I leaned in to kiss her.

As I got closer to her, something caught my eye just over her shoulder. It's hard to explain exactly what I saw; I'd never seen anything like it before. It was like it wasn't there one minute and then it was the next. It was nearly see-through, but not, and it looked as if it was coming more and more into focus. I had totally forgotten where I was and what I was about to do, all I could focus on was this, whatever it was, that seemed to be materializing behind Jess. I must have hesitated too long because I heard Jess say, "Are you okay?" She sounded like she was miles away from me, not mere inches. The words had barely come out of her mouth when a wave of pure exhaustion passed over me. It was an all-encompassing tiredness and the world started to fade away. The sides of my vision began to blur. The darkness started to creep in, slowly at first then faster and faster until I began to lose consciousness. As I passed out, I could finally see that the "shape" behind Jess, which had seemed formless at first, now had the unmistakable shape of a person. And then there was nothing but blackness.

# 17

# JESS

What was I thinking? I knew it was a mistake before I agreed to go out with him. He was a patient. I knew better than this. Even if he was technically no longer one of my patients, it was just wrong. He would be back to the hospital soon for more tests. What would the other residents think? I know they thought I was the sad girl who had no life outside of the hospital. It wouldn't help their opinion of me if I started seeing a patient, former or not. I've seen enough Grey's Anatomy to know how that turns out. But there was something about Eric. I don't know what it was but since he woke up, I haven't been able to get him off my mind. He was a miracle. I can't even believe I am saying that but that is what he was. He should be dead. He shouldn't still be alive and he sure as hell shouldn't have been asking me out on a date.

The second I said yes to his proposal, I had regrets. Not because I didn't want to go but because, I don't know, it has been nearly a decade since I've been on a date. I was so nervous I could feel my palms starting to sweat. I hoped he didn't notice. To be honest, I don't even really remember what he was saying. I was equal parts terrified and oddly at ease, because there were parts of him that reminded me so much of Jack it hurt.

And as soon as I told him that I just assumed the date would be over. No one wants to date the broken girl. But he surprised me. The fact that I had a complicated past didn't scare him off, quite the opposite actually. I think it intrigued him. For the first time in longer than I care to admit, I felt hopeful. Not that I would find someone as perfect for me as Jack, I knew that wouldn't happen, but maybe I could find someone who accepted me, warts and all.

It didn't hurt either that Eric was a very handsome guy and quite charming in that dorky, playful sort of way. In the way Jack was. But part of me thinks I'll look for similarities between Jack and any guy. He is, after all, my only frame of reference. I've loved him for almost my entire life.

When he said he was going to kiss me, in my head I was yelling, no! And I could visualize myself putting my hand up to stop him. But in reality, I couldn't make my mouth, or my hands move. So, I just closed my eyes and waited for my first kiss in close to a decade. I felt like a sixteen-

year-old waiting for the cute boy at school to ask her out to Prom. And then nothing...

I finally let my guard down a little and look what happens. As we headed to the hospital, I replayed the day in my head. Eric came to shortly after he blacked out. For a moment, only briefly I thought he had died...again. As he came to, I felt a huge sense of relief wash over me. He tried to shake it off like it wasn't a big deal but I could tell he was worried too. I know I had technically just met him yesterday, but he had been my patient for a month before he woke up. I cared about him and not just in a doctor-patient sort of way. I'd told him he reminded me of Jack but it was more than that. Even if it was fleeting, he made me feel, period. I thought that part of me died with Jack.

None of this should have happened. I hadn't expected to see Eric today. Honestly, I hadn't expected to see him at all. I told myself I wasn't going to go to any of his follow-up appointments, that my job was done. Dr. Anderson could take it from there. But then there he was as I walked up to the hospital and I have to admit that my heart did skip a beat.

The whole time we walked through the park we walked in silence. I kept trying to sneak glances at him. It had been so long since I felt anything other than sadness that I didn't want it to end. Eight years is a long time to not feel alive. But what did I really know about Eric? Nothing really, I only know what his parents told me. And as much as parents like to think they know their children, they rarely do. But there was an instant comfort with Eric that I couldn't deny. Once we sat and talked, I started to think about Jack. My instinct was to run away, to go back to my cave of an apartment and hide out from the world. In a weird way, I also felt like I was somehow cheating on Jack by spending time with someone other than him.

For so long he occupied a large part of my day. I would spend hours daydreaming about what life would be like if he were still here. Would he be proud of me becoming a doctor? Would I have even become a doctor if he were still alive? I used to think about that all the time. I started to feel super overwhelmed. But the funny thing is, Eric never looked at me like I was broken. Not even once. When I tried to run and he took my hand, I could feel his energy and see the look in his eyes. There was no pity. I'd gotten so used to that look, the "poor Jess" look that everyone

gives me. I know everyone means well, but it gets really tiresome to be constantly looked at like you are on the verge of crumbling to pieces. But that's not how Eric looked at me. He just accepted me. And when he wanted to know about Jack it didn't feel like he was prying or trying to be delicate. That's the other thing everyone thinks that if they ask about Jack I am going to have a nervous breakdown or something. The truth is, yes, it's hard to think about him sometimes, but that's just being human. I'm not made of glass though, and Eric didn't treat me like I was. Who was this guy and how did he get under my skin so fast? I know I'm repeating myself, but my thoughts are currently all jumbled up in my head.

I wonder if he was like this before his accident. I've heard stories about how people who have had near-death experiences come back completely different. What if he was an asshole before all this, and this guy sitting in front of me, this guy I found myself wanting to kiss was only temporary? But then I thought about Betty and Bob and they were good people so I assumed they would raise a good man. And then before I knew it, I was telling Eric all these things about me that I don't tell anyone like how Jack and I had wanted to go to Paris together, but we never did. I'm

never like this, my feelings are mine and I'm very private about them. But here I was spilling everything to Eric. It caught me off guard to say the least. Not as much as when he looked up into my eyes. You know those moments in movies every girl loves, and guys roll their eyes at... it was one of those moments. It was like he wasn't just looking into my eyes, he was looking into my heart, into my soul. It felt primal. It felt like the world around us stopped and slowly faded away. There was nothing but us. I could see every pore, every freckle on his face. I could see that his blue eyes had a little twinge of green in them running along the bottom of his irises. But more than that, I saw him, I could feel ourselves drawn towards each other but neither of us were moving. I was snapped back to reality by the sound of Eric hitting the ground.

My first thought was that whatever "miracle" was keeping him alive had ended. I was hoping I was wrong and selfishly I wanted to be wrong because this person, this stranger had started to bring me back to life, and I didn't want that to end. Those thoughts were all fleeting as my medical training kicked in. First, I checked his pulse—he had one! As I was about to check his airways he started to stir. I leaned down beside him and helped him sit up. He had a look I was used to seeing in the hospital. It was a mixture of confusion and fear. It only lasted for a second and he tried to hide it from me, but it was too late. Up until then I hadn't really thought about how he must have been feeling with all of this, with everyone basically telling him he should be dead. Of course, he must be scared, who wouldn't be.

I took my pen light out of my purse. "Eric, I want you to follow the light." I watched his pupillary reaction as I shone my light in both of his eyes. He followed them perfectly. Normally I would ask several questions to make sure he remembered where he was, what day it was, things like that. But I already knew Eric was still figuring all of that out. Eric tried to lighten the mood by cracking jokes about getting a little too excited about kissing me, but I could see through the act. I took his hand. "Eric, I think we should go back to the hospital. I want to run some tests, just to make sure everything is fine." My words fell on deaf ears; he was looking behind me, lost in thought. I turned around and there was nothing there. I couldn't quite place this new expression; he looked shell-shocked, a million miles away. I turned back around towards him. "What are you looking for, Eric?" But he was still on another

planet, so I snapped my fingers and called his name a little louder. That did it and he snapped out of whatever daze he was in. I softened my voice. "What are you looking for? There is nothing there, Eric." He just smiled at me again and said he was just really tired, but that same look of fear was peeking out from behind his perfect smile. I stood up and held out my hand. "Come on, let's go get you checked out." As he looked up at me the smile faded and all I saw was concern. He nodded slightly yes and put his hand in mine, and I helped him to his feet.

We walked back to the hospital pretty much in silence. Occasionally Eric would look behind us almost as if he was trying to see if someone was following us, but there never was. When we got to the hospital, I left Eric in one of the exam rooms and filled Dr. Anderson in on what just happened. She agreed that I should run some tests to make sure there wasn't something happening to Eric. I came back into the room and Eric was asleep. I tried to gently wake him. As he stirred, he looked up at me with sleepy eyes. He tried to get up. "Not so fast, mister." I carefully eased him back down on the bed. He told me he just wanted to go home and get some rest. I tried to sound as professional as possible as I told him that once we ran some tests and made

sure everything was fine he was free to go home. I don't know if I succeeded though; I feel like I sounded more like a concerned girlfriend, than his doctor. What was going on with me? What was it about Eric that was throwing me off so much?

The first test I ran was a CT Scan of Eric's body and in particular his brain to see if there were any changes. I could tell he was not happy to be back in the hospital. I couldn't blame him, whether he was conscious of it or not, he had been in this place for a really long time, so I knew how hard it must be for him. He was a trooper though and lay still the entire time. Next, I did an EKG to make sure everything was okay with his heart. Finally, I drew some blood and ordered a battery of tests that we would get the results from in a few days. As the nurse pulled out the needle from his arm, he smiled happy that the last test was finished. "So, am I all done, Doc? Do I at least get a cookie?" I smiled. Eric was quite the charmer when he wanted to be, I was coming to find out. I looked at him, my smile fading slightly. "I just need to compare these new scans to your last scans to make sure there haven't been any changes since you left the hospital." He sighed deeply and followed me into another room where our x-ray

illuminator was kept. I took the old scans and put them up against new scans that the nurse had just brought in to me. Eric sat in a nearby chair watching me intently. I first looked at the full-body scans and there was nothing out of the ordinary. Then I took a closer look at the brain scans and again I couldn't find any problems or discrepancies. I unconsciously let out a deep breath. It must have been louder than I intended because Eric laughed. "Guess I'm not dying just yet, huh, Doc?" I leaned up against the window to the hallway and looked at him and chuckled. "Yes, I think you'll make it. All your scans check out fine and your blood work should be back in a few days." Eric got up and took a couple steps towards me with a smirk. "Good then, we can pick up where we left off." The words had no sooner left his mouth than something caught his eye in the hallway behind me. His smile instantly disappeared and the same shell-shocked look from the park returned. I took a step towards him. "Eric, Eric, what do you see?" But I had lost him again. His eyes were following something moving down the hallway. I turned and looked through the window, but I saw nothing. What was he looking at? He ran out the door into the hallway and stared with his mouth agape.

# 18

# JACK

I was finally starting to calm down. Jess had run all her tests and there didn't seem to be anything wrong with me. I let out a sigh of relief. I had thought I was running out of time in this body, sooner than I had planned, but thankfully I was just being paranoid. There was a persistent exhaustion that never seemed to go away. I wondered if it had something to do with the fact that I was a passenger in this body. In a way, I was a parasite, a virus, and Eric's body was the unwilling host. I didn't want to think about it in those stark terms, but it was true. I think Jess was relieved too because I could see the tension in her shoulders letting up. All I wanted to do was walk over to her and kiss her. I knew I couldn't, this was where she worked but it took all my willpower to resist grabbing her and planting one on her. The best I could do was to get her out of there and get back our date, to remind her she was having a nice time with 'Eric'. But then I saw it again, what I had seen in the park before I passed out. It was just over her right shoulder through the window. But this time it was different, it was moving and

it looked bigger to me. I completely forgot that Jess was even in the room and I ran towards the door. Whatever it was, it passed right by me and for a moment I had the same wave of dizziness I'd had in the park.

I braced myself on the doorframe for a moment, collected myself, and then ran out into the hallway to follow. Whatever it was, it was definitely different this time. I couldn't be sure of what I was seeing because it was constantly changing, but it looked like there were three of them moving in unison together. It was still translucent at times but every now and then it would momentarily take a shape. It resembled smoke, constantly swirling, disappearing, reappearing. The shape kept changing as the three separate masses fluctuated and intertwined with each other. What the hell was going on? Could anyone else see them besides me? I don't think they could because no one seemed to be reacting as the masses moved down the corridor. Was something actually wrong with me, something medical? These thoughts were racing through my head. The mass was starting to phase in and out; I started to have trouble seeing it. I heard Jess calling for me in the distance behind me as I ran down the hallway. As I turned the corner I could hear her chasing after me. What must people be thinking of what they are

seeing? Did they think I was a runaway patient and my doctor was chasing after me? If that was the case, how long before the security guards started coming for me as well?

But those thoughts were in the distant parts of my brain, foremost was following these shapes and finding out exactly what they were. I turned the corner in pursuit and when the next hallway came into full view there was nothing there.

The shapes were gone. What happened? Where did they go?

Jess caught up with me, out of breath. "Eric, what are you doing? What are you chasing after?" I turned around and looked her in the eyes, sure that the fear I was feeling at that moment was written all over my face. I watched closely for her reaction. "You didn't see them, there were three of them." She responded, "Three what, Eric? I didn't see anything, I don't see anything, there is nothing here." My world started to get cloudy again. I wasn't going to pass out but there was a horrible realization beginning to sink in. Something was happening that only I could see. I was running out of time.

There was no way for me to be sure—it's not like I possess bodies every week—but that was the only explanation that made any sense to me. In that moment, I remember wishing that all of this, all these years, my death, every moment of it was just a bad nightmare and I was going to wake up any minute and be back in bed with Jess in our little apartment in the city. That I hadn't died, that Jess hadn't wasted eight years of her life being sad and alone, that none of it had actually happened. I closed my eyes and wished with all my might but when I opened them I, Eric, was still standing in the middle of the hallway at the hospital.

As I stood there, I felt like the hallway was starting to get longer and longer, never ending. I felt like I was in the middle of the ocean and my legs were starting to get tired and I was slowly starting to drown. I didn't know what to do next. How much time did I have? A week? A day?

An hour? A minute? Was this my last minute before Heaven figured out what I had been doing? Was this my last minute before I was punished for eternity? Visions of the nine circles of Hell from Dante's Inferno started to swirl around in my head. I was deep in my thoughts when Jess put her hand on my shoulder. She tried her best to sound calm and soothing, but her voice was on the verge of cracking when she asked, "Eric, what are you seeing? Can you explain it to me?" I tried my best to put into words what I had seen but I couldn't come up with anything that didn't make me sound crazy. She asked me if she should call Betty and Bob. I, a little too emphatically, told her no. I couldn't handle keeping up all these lies. I didn't know what to say, so I didn't say anything. I walked over to a couple of chairs set up outside a patient's room and I sat down and put my head in my hands. I felt Jess come and sit down next to me.

She put her hand on my back and gently rubbed it in a circle. That's what she used to do back in the day whenever I came home from work and was feeling really stressed out. It always calmed me down and made me smile. I slowly started to breathe a little easier, but I still had no idea what to say. Should I tell her the truth? Would she even believe me if I did? I shook that thought away, I couldn't tell her the truth, it would be too much to handle. The only thing I felt like I could tell her were my fears, that we didn't have much longer together.

I looked up at her and into those eyes, those eyes I used to stare at for hours, and I got lost like I always did. The words didn't come but they didn't need to, whether she realized it or not she could see me. That was something Jess and I always had. We always knew what the other was thinking without a word ever being spoken. It did comfort me slightly to feel that again, but it also made me feel

terrible because Jess didn't know she was feeling that again with me, with Jack, not with Eric. As far as she knew she was having that connection with someone else, someone who may or may not be dying. The longer I was in Eric's body the worse I felt about lying to Jess; it was slowly eating me up inside. But I guess I wouldn't have to worry about it too much longer. Whatever was happening with me it was getting worse. It was the first time I actually wanted to see Alistair so he could explain to me what was going on. But I couldn't, I hadn't known him for very long, but it was pretty obvious he was a stickler for the rules. How would he react if he saw what I had done? Would he turn me in? A million questions were running through my head when Jess took my hand in hers and pulled me out of my thoughts. I shook my head slightly mentally pushing all those questions I had away and reconnecting with Jess. She looked at me with concern. "I know you must be scared, Eric, but we will get to the bottom of whatever is happening to you." I tried to smile because I appreciated the sentiment, but I knew there was nothing Jess or any other doctor in this hospital would be able to do. I had gotten myself into this without thinking about the consequences and I was starting to get scared. Scared of what was going to happen to me.

And what about Jess? Would there be any consequences for her, simply by association? Would Heaven be that cruel? But then a thought occurred to me. The damage had already been done. I shouldn't be afraid, I should be embracing every single moment I had left here. I should cherish every second I had with Jess. I wasn't exactly given a second chance, I cheated and took one, but I should still make the most of it before it is gone.

I knew what I needed to do, what I wanted to do I just had to convince Jess now. I smiled slightly and asked her, "Would you go away with me?" I could tell my question caught her by surprise, but I pressed on, "Look, Jess, I don't know how much time I have left. I feel like it's running out, and I want to spend the rest of it with you." She blushed slightly and looked down. "You hardly know me, Eric, you can't mean that." I wanted to tell her the truth so badly, that I knew everything about her but I didn't. I took her hands in mine. "I'm here for a reason, Jess, and that reason is you. I know you feel the same for me, I can see it in your eyes, even if you don't realize it." She shook her head. "Even if that's true, and I'm not saying it is, you could be really sick, Eric—" I cut her off, "No one can predict the future, maybe I'm totally fine and I'm

going to live a long happy life, but just in case I'm not I want to make the most of this. If this is the end of the line for me, don't I deserve to have one more adventure?" I could see that I was starting to get through to her even if it was just a little. She looked down the hallway as if she was looking for answers. "If I were to agree to go somewhere with you, and that doesn't mean I will, where were you thinking?" She looked up at me with that little half smile that always melted me and I instantly knew exactly where we should go. A big smile came over my face. "We should go to Paris and see Oscar Wilde's tomb."

# 19

# JESS

He took me completely by surprise when he asked me to go to Paris with him. I started laughing and stood up. "I can't go to Paris! Eric, I have a job!" He stood up. "Do you have sick days?" I replied hesitantly, "Of course I do, but..." He tried to lighten things slightly. "Well, I'm sick, Jess, isn't that the whole point of sick days?" What kind of a joke is that? Eric had a really twisted sense of humor. It might have been one of the few things that I didn't like about him. "That's not funny, Eric, what if something happens and it could have been prevented if we'd just waited till your blood work came back?" How could I go on a trip with him? How many moral and ethical lines would I be crossing? But I can't lie...to finally see Paris is really tempting. Eric pushed on. "You said to me that Paris is somewhere you have always wanted to go. Now you have an opportunity. Why are you fighting it? Stop living your life in a bubble. Why are you so afraid to live your life, Jess!" The words spilled out of his mouth and hit me like a sledgehammer.

I took a step towards him; I could feel my rage building. "Who the hell do you think you are! You know nothing about me, Eric! And how dare you presume to know how I am living my life! I knew this was a mistake, thank you for proving that to me." And with that I started to walk down the hallway. I heard him running after me, so I stopped. I could barely contain my anger. It hurt more than I realized. He skidded to a halt in front of me and fell on his sword. "Jess, I'm so sorry for what I said, I didn't mean for it to come out that way. All I meant was that you deserve to have some happiness in your life. And I know you feel something for me whether you want to admit it to yourself or not." My anger started to ebb, and it was replaced by sadness. Was he right? How did this guy that I barely knew figure out exactly who I was in just a couple of days? Am I that transparent? For a brief moment, I was ready to put him in his place again but then the realization hit me that he was right. He softened his tone. "Jess, can I ask you a question? I hope this doesn't upset you because that is not my intention, but have you even been on a date with anyone since Jack passed?" He then crossed the hallway without any hesitation, put his hands on either side of my face, and kissed me. I was completely taken aback but it felt right, and I didn't want it to end. It was the spark that opened the floodgates that I had kept

closed for so long. I couldn't keep the tears in anymore. We kissed for what felt like an eternity. Before I could speak, he made a proposition. "How about this, I will be at the airport tomorrow at one o'clock with two tickets to Paris, one for me and one for you. I hope you change your mind and decide to come with me." He kissed me on the cheek and walked away before I could say anything.

I wanted to just scream yes and leave with him that minute, but how could I? I had a job and a life here, I couldn't just drop it all and run away with a guy I didn't know, even if he did seem to know the real me. And the truth is, I was absolutely terrified, terrified to open myself up to someone new, to really feel again. What if it didn't work out? What if it did work out and he was taken away from me again, just like Jack was? I wouldn't be able to survive that again. I probably stood in the hallway for a good twenty minutes in a complete fog. I had no idea what to do.

On the one hand, it was Paris, a place I have always wanted to go, and the gesture was one of the most romantic moments of my life. What girl wouldn't want a guy who goes out of his way to sweep her off her feet? But on the other hand, Paris was my dream with Jack, was I ready to let that dream die? Also, was I really ready to open myself up to someone who wasn't Jack. I don't know, but I did know how Eric made me feel. And then there was Eric's health. Was everything okay with him or was time running out? Was his grand gesture really about me or was he trying to cross one last thing off his bucket list just in case his number was up soon, for good this time? These were all thoughts running through my head and they made me feel happy, sad, confused, awful, and a million other feelings all at the same time.

I made my way back to the Residents' Lounge and searched through my locker for my phone. I called Andrea because I needed some advice. When she heard the sound of my voice, she was instantly worried, and we agreed to meet for dinner that night to discuss things. I honestly don't even know what I did with myself for the next few hours; it was all a blur. When I eventually walked into the restaurant to meet Andrea she was of course on time and already had a table waiting for us. She had that look on her face, the "here comes broken Jess" face where her head tilts slightly to one side and she does her best to not have a concerned expression—she failed every time. She put her arms around me and gave me a big hug that lasted just a bit too long for my liking. I know it sounds like I didn't

like her, but that's not true, she was one of the kindest people I knew, and she helped me get through everything more than I even think she realized. I just wish sometimes she wouldn't look at me like I was barely hanging on by a string, even though I clearly was. She held on to my hand as we sat down at the table. "Sooo...how are things, Jess?" I just started laughing, I'm not even sure why, maybe it was because I couldn't answer a simple question like that, but my laughter quickly turned to tears and I started sobbing at the table. Ugh, I've officially become one of those girls I used to make fun of, crying over some guy...in public, but I couldn't help it. Andrea said nothing all she did was hold my hand until I finished crying. Andrea smiled at me and handed me her napkin. "Do you maybe want to start at the beginning?" And as if on cue, the waiter walked over with two bottles of red wine, one for each of us—God, I love Andrea! I put my hand on top of hers and she smiled. "I figured it was going to be a two-bottle kind of night."

After the waiter uncorked both bottles of wine and filled our glasses I raised mine to toast with Andrea, but the standard cheers didn't really seem to apply. There was only one word that kept floating around in my head, so I went with that. "To miracles." Andrea looked a little confused but we clinked glasses anyway. I started, "So there is this patient of mine who has been in a coma after a skiing accident..." "Did he pass away?" I shook my head and Andrea looked intrigued. "He was brain dead. There was nothing more we could do to help him, so I talked to his parents and made them understand that their son was gone. Since he had a DNR, his wishes were to not live a life hooked up to machines." Andrea took a big swig of her wine. "That's awful, I don't know how you do that. How did they take it?" I took a deep breath. "Not well. Betty, his mom, didn't believe he was gone. She kept saying that she had prayed Eric would be okay, and she was convinced her prayers were going to be answered. Eventually her husband Bob had to explain to her what was going on and that turning off the machines was what their son would have wanted." Andrea looked like the she was going to cry when she said, "I can't even imagine having to say goodbye to my child like that. Did it take long for him to pass?" I skipped the sipping and downed my glass of wine and chuckled. "That's the thing, we turned off all the machines and waited for him to pass but then he woke up!" Andrea slammed her hand down on the table a little harder than she realized, and it startled me and the table next to us.

"Sorry, wait, how did he wake up?" I shrugged my shoulders. "I have no idea, Andrea. Medically, he was dead, he should be dead, but he isn't, he is just walking around now.

Breathing, talking, living. I can't explain it. We ran every test I could think of and there is nothing medically wrong with him now. The swelling in his brain? It's gone. It is a..."

I could see the light bulb go off in her head before I got the words out. "A miracle. Do you think his mother's prayers were answered?" "I have absolutely no idea. Betty is convinced God heard her prayers and brought her son back, but I believe in science, I believe in what I can see and prove. I can't just take something on faith. It brings up too many questions. Why him? What is so special about this guy, this situation? Why not someone else? Why not Jack?" I paused, realizing there was a part of me that was upset or jealous that he was able to come back and Jack wasn't. Andrea could tell I didn't want to go down that path so she redirected the conversation. "No wonder you are a little emotional." I poured more wine. "You have no idea, that is just the beginning, there is so much more I need to tell you." Andrea followed suit and filled up her glass. "Did something else happen?" I filled her in on all the medical details, about his amnesia but I hesitated for a minute before going into everything else, I didn't really know how to start. I hadn't talked to Andrea about a guy— since Jack. It felt a little strange, but I pushed on. "So, the other morning I was walking to work and Eric was waiting for me outside the hospital. I should probably back up and say that he had been flirting with me pretty much from the moment he woke up, and even though it made me uncomfortable, it was also really nice. Anyway, he convinced me to go get coffee with him in the park. He just grabbed my hand and that was that."

Andrea's eyes lit up, I could only imagine she had been waiting a really long time to hear me talk about something or someone other than Jack. Her enthusiasm made me blush slightly, but I continued, "We barely said a word as we walked through the park together, we were just like every other couple holding hands. It was so easy and simple. It felt the way it used to feel with Jack, it was uncomplicated. There is something so familiar, so comforting about him. It's strange, but I feel like he knows me. I told him things I never tell anyone, things about Jack, about how we wanted to go to Paris together before he died." Andrea was a little shocked. She knew how

I kept most of those things to myself. "And what happened next?" I sighed "Well, we almost kissed, but then something happened. Just before he kissed me it was like he saw a ghost. Next thing I knew, he'd passed out." Andrea gasped, "Oh my God, is he okay?"

I told her about how Eric had seen "something" in the hallway and chased after it and how worried I was that there was something wrong with him we just didn't know what. Andrea looked confused. "Did you see anything?" I fiddled with my wine glass for a minute. "There was nothing there, I don't know what he saw, or what he thinks he saw, but it's in his head. And I think he is scared and doesn't want to admit that he knows something is wrong too."

Andrea grabbed my hand. "No wonder you are stressed out, Jess, that all sounds really scary." I looked up at the ceiling and put my face in my hands. "That isn't everything, there is more."

Andrea didn't believe me. "How is there more? What else happened?" I whispered it because there was a part of me that didn't think it was real. "He asked me to go to Paris with him." Andrea's eyes bulged out of her head. "What? What did you say?" I told her everything about us fighting in the hallway me crying and him kissing me and I

could see Andrea hanging on my every word. "How did things end?" she asked. "Well, that's what I need your advice on. "He told me he would be waiting at the airport tomorrow with two tickets to Paris and that he hoped I would go with him. And then he kissed me on the cheek and left."

Andrea called to the waiter, "I think we are going to need more wine!" The waiter returned shortly with another bottle and Andrea filled us up. "Do you know what you want to do?" I admitted to her that I had absolutely no idea what I wanted to do. Andrea thought for a moment and then asked me, "What would you do if Jack had asked you to go on a last-minute trip to Paris?" I didn't even have to think about it. "Of course I would go, no questions asked." Andrea gave me a, , look and said, "The real question is, do you want to go with Eric? I know he's not your Jack, Jess, and he never will be, but what if he could be your Eric? From what you told me he seems like a great guy and he is obviously crazy about you. So, what's holding you back?" I guess I already knew the reason, I just didn't want to say it out loud, but Andrea had done her job well and I was well liquored up by that point. I took a deep breath. "What if he dies?" Andrea downed the last of her glass of wine and took both of my hands in

hers. "Honey, you've been afraid of that for long enough, no one knows when their time is up. For all you know, Eric could live a long healthy life and you could die tomorrow." She signed the cross like any good former Catholic schoolgirl would before continuing, "You have to stop letting your life pass you by. I know it's been hard, and I don't know how I would have handled losing the love of my life but, Jess, that was eight years ago. Don't you think you have mourned long enough? Don't you think you deserve to be happy? Let me ask you this. What would Jack want you to do?" That last line hit me like a ton of bricks and I started to tear up. "He would want me to be happy." Andrea continued, emptying the last bit of bottle number three into my glass, "And does Eric make you happy?" I nodded yes and downed the glass. She smiled. "Well, then you better get out of here and start packing, you're going to Paris in the morning!" She made it all seem so clear. Honestly, I felt a little stupid that I hadn't been able to put that all together myself, but maybe three bottles of wine and my best friend was what I needed to make a decision. I hugged her, and we settled the bill and stumbled out of the restaurant. As we crashed onto the street an elderly couple gave us that look all old people have perfected, the

'disappointed grandparent' look. In their defense they weren't wrong, we were embarrassing. I tried to hail a cab as Andrea yelled at them to mind their own business, moments before she fell into the planters in front of the restaurant.

# 20

# JACK

I woke up early in the morning because I couldn't sleep, there were so many thoughts running through my head. Would Jess come meet me at the airport? Would she stand me up? If she did, what did I do next? Would I just give up and head back? Or would I try harder to get through to her? And what was happening in Heaven? By now they had to have known what was happening, they had to be working on a way to rectify the situation. How would it happen? Would I just cease to be? Or would I be in Hell before I even realized what was happening, before I had a chance to say goodbye to Jess? And where was Alistair? I had last seen him when I was entering Eric's body. Could I not see him anymore?

The more I thought about Alistair, the more I was glad that maybe there was a chance I couldn't see him. I had so many questions that I wasn't sure I wanted the answers to. What were the things I had been seeing, those gray swirling figures only I was able to see? Where did they come from?

Why couldn't Jess, or anyone else for that matter, see them? Also, why was I so incredibly tired all the time? I know Alistair would not approve of what I had done, and

more and more I was starting to feel the same way, but it's too late to go back now. I had to see this through, whatever the outcome was. Hindsight is twenty-twenty, as they say. All of those thoughts were running through my head as I showered and got dressed.

I had called Betty and Bob the night before to tell them my plan, it seemed like the right thing to do, I mean what if something happened to me, to Eric in Paris and they never had a chance to say goodbye. Would they be able to recover from losing their son a second time? Betty couldn't hide her fear. She didn't think it was safe for me to go.

It broke my heart. She just got her son back. Her fears made perfect sense, but it also made me feel like a complete monster. Who was I becoming? They wanted to come and have breakfast before I left. I reluctantly agreed.

After we spoke, I started to pack for Paris. While I looked through Eric's closets and drawers, my mind once again started to wander back to the previous day in the hospital with Jess and to those, I don't even know what word to use, "things" that I saw in the hallway. These were different than what I had seen in the park. I was certain there were three distinct shapes this time. These thoughts were all

circling through my head when Betty called for me from the kitchen to come eat, she had been cooking while I packed.

I walked into the kitchen and the smell of bacon and eggs and waffles nearly knocked me over. Betty stood with a Statue of David apron tied around her waist. It was an interesting sight to say the least. Clearly Eric had a sense of humor when he was alive. Betty came over and gave me a kiss on the cheek. Her fears were still written all over her face, but she did her best to cover them with a cheerful smile. "Good morning, honey, I hope you're hungry, it's a long flight to Paris." Even though I didn't know them from Adam, I have to admit, it was nice to sit with them and have breakfast. Betty made me a heaping plate of food and I tucked in. "So are you excited for the trip? Do you know what you two are going to do?" I took a minute to finish chewing what was in my mouth. Wow, it was good! I wanted to tell Betty she should open a restaurant but for all I knew she might already have. It was getting harder and harder to keep up the charade and part of me wished I could just tell them the truth, but I knew I couldn't. I smiled at Betty. "Well, first off, I'm just hoping Jess shows up." Betty looked at me intently. "Of course she will show up, Eric, you just have to have faith." There was that

word again—faith. She based so much purely on faith, I wish I had an ounce of the conviction she did, the truth was I was starting to feel more and more sure that Jess wasn't going to show up. The Jess I knew when I was alive, well that was a different story, she would be there without a doubt. But this Jess, she was lonely, sad and afraid, and she had been that way for so long that I wasn't sold on her being able to remember the person she used to be. I didn't have faith, but I did have hope. I guess that is better than nothing. Bob chimed in, "And how are you feeling, son?" Thankfully Jess had listened to me and hadn't called Betty and Bob yesterday to tell them I passed out in the park. I didn't want to worry them anymore than they already were. They had already tried their best to talk me out of going. I felt bad but if they knew they would stop me from going to Paris with Jess and this might be my last chance, so what was one more lie, in the grand scheme of things.

This is what I kept telling myself to hopefully keep the growing sense of dread at bay. I know what I was doing was wrong, but what is done is done, right? And today I was feeling better so when I told him that I wasn't lying.

Through the rest of breakfast, we talked about some things to do in Paris. Jess and I had never gotten around to

planning the trip, other than wanting to see where Oscar Wilde was buried so I wasn't entirely sure what else Jess would want to do, I just figured we would play it by ear, assuming she even showed up at the airport in the first place. I looked up at the clock and it was getting close to noon. The morning had just flown by. Eric was a lucky guy when he was alive, Betty and Bob were really wonderful people. It only made me feel that much worse that I was lying to them about being their son. I helped clear the dishes and finished packing up the last of my bag. As I was getting ready to leave Betty came over and gave me a big hug and she held me tight for much longer than an average hug would have lasted. Her actions finally betrayed her fears. She may have faith in a lot of things, but she is still a human being and a mother, and from the way she held me I knew there was a part of her that was worried she was never going to see her son again. She might be right. When she let me go her eyes were glistening. She tried to wipe her eyes so I wouldn't see them, but it was too late. So, I did what I thought Eric would have done. I gave her a kiss on the cheek and said, "I love you, Mom." I waved goodbye to Bob and I was out the door, feeling like the worst former human being inhabiting the body of another human being on the planet.

# 21

# BETTY

I've been a bundle of nerves ever since Eric woke up. I had asked him to take it easy, but Eric has always been stubborn. He's always been a good son but when that boy wants to do something there really isn't much that is going to stop him. He got that from his father. With everything he has been through in the last month I wanted him to rest and let us take care of him. I can't say I blame him though for wanting to get on with his life. God granted him a second chance and he has made it pretty clear he is not going to waste it. But I'm his mother, it is my job to worry. It is my job to protect him and to keep him safe.

Dr. Miller ran every test she could think of and they found nothing wrong with Eric. He is still having trouble with his memory, but the doctors are hopeful that in time his memory will come back to him. Even if it never came back, I had my Eric back and that was all that mattered. I've been trying to remain positive and not let negative thoughts enter my head but there is a part of me that is waiting for the bottom to drop out again.

The only people who knew where we were staying were the doctors at the hospital and Eric. When I heard the phone ring I thought, only for a moment, that something worse had happened to Eric. I was so relieved to hear his voice on the other end of the line. "Hi, honey, how are you feeling? Is everything okay?" He assured me that everything was fine. Unconsciously, I let out a sigh of relief. He told me about his plan to go to Paris with Dr. Miller the following day. I guess if my son is going to start dating her, I should get used to calling her Jess. Truthfully, I don't think he should go. He just came out of a month-long coma less than a week ago, he should be resting. I could tell even he had concerns that coming back to life might be temporary.

That terrifies me to even say out loud and it's another reason why I don't want him to go. I would never forgive myself if something happened to him and I didn't get to say goodbye. I needed to make sure he was back to his old self. Since he woke up there is something different about him. I can't put my finger on it, it's something I just feel. The doctors told me we needed to be patient with him, that no one has woken up after suffering the kinds of injuries Eric had. Honestly, I don't think they knew what was happening with him. But a mother just knows. Hopefully, in time Eric will feel more like himself but until then I needed to let him figure things out for himself, as much as I wanted to do it for him and make him all better. I can't do that. I tried to tell him it wasn't a good idea, but he wouldn't budge. Eric has been stubborn since he was a kid. Once he's made up his mind about something it's nearly impossible to change his mind. So, I lied to him and told him I was happy for him to go to Paris and how romantic I thought it would be. He wanted us to come over in the morning and have breakfast before he goes to the airport.

After I hung up the phone, I told Bob what Eric was planning and that I wanted to go to church to light some candles and pray. It just made me feel better and I felt like I needed to make sure God heard my prayers for Eric.

When we got to Eric's apartment in the morning, he was a mix of excitement and nerves. It reminded me of how Eric was on Christmas

Eve. He could barely contain his excitement that Santa Claus was going to be coming to the house later. He wanted to stay up and meet him, but he also didn't want him to think he was a bad boy, sneaking up at night to see Santa putting his presents out. He would sit in bed and pretend to be asleep. It was the cutest thing, but he wasn't fooling anyone. No one sleeps with a big Cheshire grin on his face.

I made breakfast while Eric finished getting ready. There was something different about Eric this morning. He felt just a little bit more like his old self. He seemed more carefree than he had yesterday. Maybe the doctors were right, it was just going to take time for Eric to fully come back to us. He was here in body, I guess it would just take a little longer for him to be here in spirit. God was continuing to hear my prayers. We sat down to breakfast and it felt like old times. Eric was coming back to us and he deserved to do whatever he felt like doing.

After breakfast, he finished up the last of his packing and I tried my best to keep from crying but I was never good at hiding my emotions. I hugged him and didn't want to let go. I had faith that he was going to be okay on his trip. I had faith that God would watch over him and protect him, but he is my only son and I just got him back. It's a mother's job to worry and I'd perfected it over the years. Usually, Eric would pull away from a hug, but this time he let me hold him tight as long as I wanted. Watching him walk out the door to the airport was easier than I thought, but I said a quick prayer for his safety just in case. One can never be too careful, right?

## 22

## JACK

I rode in the taxi to the airport in silence, trying my best to shake off the awful feelings I had because of breakfast with Eric's parents. Why had I called her Mom? How is she going to react if or when she finds out the truth? In life, I hated to lie to people, and in death it seemed that was all I did. It's not what I thought the afterlife would be, that's for sure. I didn't recognize the selfish person that I have become. I pushed those feelings down as the airport terminal came into view. As I got out of the taxi my heart starting pounding, I don't think I have been that nervous since I saw Jess walk through the door all those years ago in high school. I was hoping Jess would be there waiting for me with a big smile on her face that would put all my worries to bed, but she wasn't there.

   I looked at the clock and it was 12:55pm, this would be the longest five minutes of my life. I walked over and grabbed a coffee from the airport Starbucks hoping it would help pass the time, but it didn't. Waiting in line I just stared at the clock counting the seconds. Time was barely moving. Einstein's Theory of Relativity was proving to be very accurate. Waiting those five little minutes was near agony. I managed to distract myself briefly while I put some sugar and cream in my coffee, then I looked back up at the clock and my heart sank. It was

1:02pm and Jess was nowhere to be found.

I could almost hear my heart break. I had no plan B. This was my one shot to get through to her and it had failed. I felt lost, I felt like screaming, I felt like throwing my coffee against the wall as hard as I could. How could I have been such a fool? How could I have done all this for nothing? I was so deep in my despair that I didn't hear my name being called out. I finally turned around and there she was, my Jess, smiling at me the way she used to before all of this happened. I welled up with tears before I even realized it. She put her bag down and wrapped her hands around me. "Why are you crying?" I sniffled and tried to laugh it off, but it wasn't the time for jokes. "I thought you weren't coming." She smiled and wiped a tear from under my left eye. "I got stuck in traffic, it's New York, it happens." God, I missed how she could always make me feel better with just a couple of words. I smiled back at her and looked down at our hands as they intertwined, then back up at her and deep into her eyes. "Hi," I said.

She replied in kind and then I leaned in and kissed her slowly. If only you could choose which moments to apply to Einstein's theory; this was definitely one I wished would last longer. When we separated, we just stared at each other and smiled. "Are you ready for an adventure, Jess?" Her smile grew three times bigger. "Oui, monsieur." My smile grew to match hers. As I reached to grab her bag I glanced across the terminal and saw the last person on Earth I wanted to see in that moment—Alistair. I tried to hide my shocked expression and I must have succeeded because Jess didn't react. Why was he here now? Was he here to take me back? I'd come too far for things to end like this. I had to hope there was some way to convince him to give me more time, just a little more time is all I needed. I needed Jess to leave so I could talk to him. I turned back to her. "How about you go ahead and get us all checked in, I am just going to run to the bathroom really quick before we go through security." Jess nodded, and I gave her Eric's passport. She

## JACK

walked off towards the check-in desk. I walked in the other direction towards Alistair and an uncertain fate.

# 23

# JESS

Waking up this morning I felt like I got hit by a bus. I loved Andrea when we were three bottles of wine in, but I usually hated Andrea in the morning. This morning was no exception. But, by the looks of Andrea she was already suffering enough. She had somehow managed to pass out on the couch, sort of. Her legs were up on the back of the couch and her head was dangling precariously off the edge. She also looked as if she had been mildly electrocuted because almost every hair on her head was sticking out in a different direction. Her left knee had a scrape on it, probably from when she took a header into the bushes. I snapped a quick picture of her, I never miss an opportunity for future blackmail, especially when it comes to Andrea.

I hopped in the shower and felt almost human when I got out. I finished up packing for the airport, pretty much lost in thought the entire time. Am I crazy for doing this? That is the one question that kept popping up over and over again. This isn't me. I'm not the spontaneous girl, not anymore at least. But there was something about Eric I was just drawn to and I wanted to see where this was all going.

If nothing else came of it, I would finally get to see Paris, the city I had dreamed about seeing for so long.

I tried to be as quiet as possible as I walked out the door but who am I kidding I could have dropped a bomb and Andrea wouldn't have moved. And this wasn't the first time I'd left my apartment with Andrea still passed out inside. She would find her way to her apartment eventually. But I'm not completely heartless. I left a plate of cold pizza on the coffee table for her, pineapple and pepperoni. I thought it was disgusting but it was her favorite. Fruit does not belong on pizza.

Once I got downstairs, I hailed a cab and headed off to the airport. As soon as I got in the car though it just felt wrong. All the confidence and excitement I had been feeling when I was getting ready, left me, and all that remained was a hundred reasons why I shouldn't get on that plane with him. I'm scared. It's as simple as that.

Eric is this anomaly in my life, something that doesn't fit with the life I had resigned myself to having. Of course, I would be sad. Of course, I would be lonely.

But plenty of people spend their entire lives alone and they are just fine. I would have my patients to take care of and my friends, well, friend, to spend time with. It

would be a small life, but it could still be a good one. I got too wrapped up in this romantic idea of falling in love in Paris. That isn't what happens to someone like me. My cards have been dealt already. I had that and I lost it. It was time to make peace with that. I took a deep breath and spoke to the taxi driver. "Excuse me, sir, can you turn around please?" He looked at me in the rearview mirror and answered in a thick New York accent, "You sure, lady?" I just nodded and looked back out the window.

He took a right at the next block to head back to my apartment. This was the right decision. I'm making the right choice here. It's safer to just go home. It's smarter to not risk the life that I have now. I felt confident in my decision as I watched the buildings go by. The stress and anxiety I had been feeling all morning started to leave me and I knew I was doing the right thing. The taxi pulled up to the corner and we waited for a break in the traffic to make a right-hand turn. While we waited, I looked at the restaurant on the corner. It was your typical run of the mill New York diner. There was a couple in the corner having breakfast. They were in their late sixties if I had to hazard a guess, they looked pretty adorable. It made me think of Jack. We would have been adorable old people but

it wasn't meant to be. It did make me smile to picture him as an old man. It was the first time I had ever felt that way when I thought about Jack. I wasn't sad. And then I looked up and saw it. The sign over the restaurant, 'Price's Deli', Jack's last name.

The second I looked at the sign I was hit with one overwhelming feeling. Everything crystallized in my head. And that thought was simple: "Jess, you're an idiot!" Running away from something potentially amazing is not being safe, it's being a coward. That isn't who I am, it isn't who I used to be anyway. And that isn't who Jack would want me to be. He wouldn't want me to end up some sad old spinster lady with too many cats and not enough human interaction in her life. What am I doing? I hope there is still time to avoid making what might be the biggest mistake of my life. I snapped back to reality. "Excuse me, sir, I'm going to need you to turn this car around again and get me to the airport as quickly as possible." I could tell he was about to put up a fight and I had no time for that. I reached into my purse and pulled out a one-hundred- dollar bill and plastered it on the plexiglass that separated us. "You get me there in time and George Washington here is all yours." He chuckled to himself.

"Whatever you say, lady!" Before I even had time to say thank you, he whipped the taxi around in the middle of the street. I let out a scream or maybe it was a squeal but either way we were on our way to the airport at warp speed!

I looked at my watch as we pulled onto the airport loop, it was a few minutes to one, I made it. My driver pulled the taxi over and I got out as quickly as I could. I gave him the hundred-dollar bill like I promised and ran towards the terminal. I stopped just outside to try and gather my thoughts but who am I kidding, my brain was all jumbled. I looked down at my watch again and it was now a couple minutes past one. I took a deep breath and walked into the airport. I did my best to appear calm. I stood in the terminal and looked around. It was a pretty busy day at the airport as passengers were hustling in all directions to check in for their flights.

I saw him across the terminal. He had his back to me. I started walking over to him as he turned around. He had tears in his eyes. Seeing him and his vulnerability, I knew I was making the right decision. When I got to him, he pretended he wasn't crying. It turns out he thought I had stood him up. In a weird way seeing him cry made me feel really good. It's nice to know I still have that effect on

guys, even after all these years. I told Eric I would check us in so he could run to the bathroom before we went through security. I watched him walk towards the bathroom and I headed over to the check-in desk. As I handed the ticket agent our passports, I couldn't help but smile.

After all these years I was finally going to get to see Paris.

## 24

## ALISTAIR

Nothing short of the fate of existence hangs in the balance. It is an impossibility for a mere Guardian Angel, or even an Angel for that matter, to fully grasp the gravity of the events occurring. Only God himself can truly understand. As the Chorus of Angels explained the situation, a heaviness filled my being, that I had never encountered before. Humanity, Divinity, Heaven, Hell, Earth; would all ending unless Jack chooses to make things right again. How would he handle the truth? The truth that he alone would save or end it all. The weight of the Universe was soon on his shoulders.

I returned to Earth in search of Jack. I was still unable to sense his presence. With his soul encapsulated within a body that is not his own, the usual connection between a Guardian Angel and his ward is not active. The longer the Gates of Heaven remained closed, the worse the repercussions would be for him and for humanity as a whole. Even though every living thing has a specific destiny and Fate has a role to play in all, God granted humanity Free Will and thusly not even the Chorus of Angels could foresee

what Jack was willing to do to be with Jess. With no manner of tracking Jack, I had decided I would do the next best thing—I would follow his soulmate in hopes that he would reveal his true self to her sooner rather than later. I found her in a restaurant with her mate Andrea. From the look of things, they had imbibed several bottles of wine with no signs of slowing down. As I approached the table, they were deep in discussion about whether or not Jess should go to Paris with a young man named Eric. Perhaps this "Eric" was really Jack. In life, it was always his dream to go to Paris with Jess, maybe that is what he came back to do. Though she seemed torn, in the end Jess decided she would go with him to Paris.

I watched as Jess fretted over what to pack changing her mind multiple times as women oft do, but there was another form of distress written all over her face, guilt. Jess walked over to the couch and turned on the television and began to play the old movie she played almost every night, however the most interesting thing happened. She paused the video on a shot of Jack. He was glancing towards the camera and it gave the impression that he was looking through the television directly at her. She took a deep breath and began to speak, "Hey, Jack, there is something I

want to talk to you about. I sort of met someone and he invited me to go with him to Paris tomorrow." Jess paused and stared at the television waiting for a reply from the image on the screen. There wasn't one of course but I could see she was making the narrative up in her head anyway. She continued, responding to the imaginary side of the conversation that she had attributed to Jack, "I hope that you are okay with this. I feel like you would be. Honestly, I think you'd like him. In a weird way, he reminds me a lot of you. He seems really kind and a little strange, but so were you. I really wish you were here; I miss you so much, but I think it's finally time for me to move on. I think I'm ready. And with everything Eric has been through, he could use a vacation too." This peaked my interests. What had Eric been through? Again, Jess paused "listening" to Jack's response. She continued, "Well he nearly died, he should have died, he did die! I don't know, I'm still not entirely sure what happened, I just know he is still here, and I can't explain why. Who knows, maybe it is a miracle!" She barely got the sentence out before she started laughing, but it was no laughing matter. I felt fairly certain that Eric was not in fact Eric, but Jack. How could he have done something so cavalier! The severity of

consequences that resulted from possession were severe enough. But he had prevented a soul from crossing over. It was an unforgivable crime. I had to hope that when I confronted him he would see the error of his ways before things were irreparably damaged.

In the morning Jess spent hours trying on outfits and fixing her hair so that everything was perfect. She clearly wanted to make a good impression. I had a feeling that none of it mattered as her first impression happened many years ago. She glanced at the clock and ran out the door. On the way to the airport she nervously fiddled with the straps on her suitcase and stared out the window. She was wracked with emotion as she turned the taxi around to head home.

She eventually regained her courage and turned back around towards the airport. Upon arrival, she stood outside the terminal for several minutes trying to gather her thoughts and calm her nerves.

I was still unable to sense Jack's presence so I wasn't entirely sure how I would be able to accurately deduce that Jack was in fact who she was here to meet. She took one last deep breath and walked through the automatic doors into the airport terminal.

She looked around briefly and didn't seem to see who she was looking for. It was only momentary, but a look of doubt stretched across her face. It melted quickly when she saw whom she was there to meet. She walked over to the nearby coffee shop and I did not follow, but rather observed. If it really was Jack in the body of this young man I would know soon enough as he would be the only person there who would be able to see me. I could no longer hear what they were saying but I could tell by the chemistry between them that they were both very happy to see each other. That all changed when the young man looked across the terminal right at me, and his smile immediately vanished. In that instant, I knew for sure it was Jack.

He said something to her, and she walked off towards the nearest airline counter as he walked with purpose across the terminal towards me. He nodded towards the corner that was nearly out of view and I obliged and headed in that direction. As he got closer the look of determination on his face that was masking his fear began to fade. He stopped a few feet from me. "Why are you here, Alistair? Are you here to take me back? Did they send you? Is my time up?" He was more than just scared he was terrified. All the outrage I had been feeling up until that

point dissipated, he really had no idea of the magnitude of what he has done. I spoke in a metered tone, "I cannot bring you back, Jack, you chose this path and it is only you who can chose to end it. But I implore you to think about what you are doing. There are powers and forces at work here beyond your comprehension. You are disrupting a very careful balance and there are consequences, very severe consequences." He continued, his voice cracking slightly, "Am I going to Hell?" I shook my head slightly. "I'm afraid it is far more complicated than that."

I had expected a much different conversation, a father lecturing an unruly child, but that is not how things were unfolding. There was no malice on his part. I needed him to fully understand his dilemma. He pleaded with me, "I just need a little more time and then I will end this." These are the moments where I wished that I were corporeal so that I could take him by the shoulders and shake some sense into him. I started, "Jack, you must end this now, every moment that you continue down this path, things will continue to spiral and not just for you, for everyone." He looked at me confused. "What do you mean for everyone?" I continued, "Has it started yet?" He shook his head. "Has what started?" I took a step closer to him. "Have you started to see them yet?" I could tell by his reaction that he had, that he knew what I was talking about. "What are they?"

I had to be as clear as possible now so that he understood the gravity of his indiscretions. "Jack, you have violated God's laws. You have violated the Laws of Heaven. As a result of your arrogance, the Heavenly Gates have closed!" He looked more confused than shocked. "What do you mean the Gates are closed?" I explained, "It means it has been decreed that until you leave this body and return to Heaven to face judgment, souls cannot cross over and enter Heaven. That is what you are seeing the beginnings of. With nowhere to go they remain here, on this plane, in this realm." His eyes widened. I continued, "Innocent souls are suffering because of your choices. And it has just begun. The longer you remain and the souls are unable to crossover, the more there will be. Eventually there will be a tipping point where they won't just be visible to you." He started, "You mean—" I interjected, "Yes, they will start to become visible to Humans as well. Jack, if people began to see the souls of their recently departed loved ones. Many would believe the end times were upon them. It would be chaos, anarchy, Jack. Now imagine it

not just happening here but in every corner of the world all at once. You could be responsible for the end of humanity...the end of everything. Please, I implore you to think about what you are doing!" I could see that it was too much for him to process. "That can't be true because when I was in the Human Resources vault I saw births and deaths far past today. If this is all predetermined, wouldn't these events also be in the Human Resources vault? What about Destiny and Fate?" I shook my head, "Jack, those are irrelevant now. God also gave humans Free Will; you have chosen to take these actions. You have chosen a new path. Nothing about the future is set in firm, you are in uncharted waters now. Alas, you can choose to end this." He was scared but he was also getting angry, perhaps at me or perhaps at the situation he found himself in. I glanced across the terminal and Jess was still in line at the ticket counter, but she was nearing the front. I did not have much longer to get through to him. And to make matters worse, in the middle of the terminal I could see a collection of souls becoming visible, and as my vision widened, they began to appear throughout the terminal. I turned my attention back to our conversation. "Jack, I beg you, look around you, can't you see that it is getting

worse?" He turned to look and I could see his eyes as they clocked the souls scattered all around us. He turned back with a look of anger on his face. "Alistair, you are doing that on purpose!" "I promise you that I am not. You will see that things will only get worse. You are a Guardian Angel who has broken his vows."

I had struck a nerve. "I'm not a Guardian Angel, Alistair, I'm just a man, a man who loves that woman and deserves to have more time with her! It's not fair! I was a good person, why was I taken so soon? Why doesn't God think we deserved to be together?" "Jack, we aren't meant to understand God's intentions—" He cut me off, "No! That is what people say when something really terrible happens, but it doesn't explain anything, people just say that, so they don't end up hating God because he has a 'plan'. Well, you know what, I'm making my own plan! I am going to get on that plane with Jess, and I am going to finish this. You said it yourself there is nothing that you can do about it. It is my choice, and I am choosing to live. I am choosing Jess!" And with that he turned and walked away from me, ending the conversation. I had intended to talk sense into him but I had the opposite effect. He had to choose to end this. I had to have faith that in the end he would come to

his senses and end this before it was too late. But I fear that time is approaching rapidly. I watched as he met up with Jess, and they walked hand in hand onto the plane. I had failed.

## 25

## JACK

As we took off my mind was a thousand miles away still processing everything Alistair had told me. I had gotten what I wanted, Jess was snuggled up next to me on our way to Paris, but at what cost? I didn't want to believe I was the cause of what was happening and what would happen in the future. It had to be some kind of trick to try and get me to come back. Alistair was a goody two-shoes so I expected him to do everything in his power to try and bring me back and look like the hero, even if it was at my expense. But there was something in his eyes, in the way he looked at me. I wasn't the only one who was scared. I tried to forget that look on his face, but it was burned into my mind. What if he was telling the truth? What if because of my actions all of those innocent souls are suffering? I couldn't help but focus on all those people who deserved to cross over and weren't allowed to, because of me. And did they know what was happening to them? Or were they just wandering around lost and confused?

It made me think of the river Styx from Greek Mythology. For those who did not go to Elysium the afterlife was a dreary existence. Those who could not afford passage across the river by the Ferryman Charon were doomed to spend an eternity floating in a sea of nothingness or wandering the shores of Styx for one hundred years. In Ancient Greece, it was such a fear that the deceased were buried with coins over their eyes or in their mouths to pay Charon for safe passage across the river Styx to the Underworld.

Is that what is happening now? With nowhere to go, were these innocent souls doomed to just wander the Earth until I ended this? Were they trapped in limbo? What if Jess were one of those lost souls, how would I react? The thought of that made me feel disgusted with myself. How am I capable of this? How selfish of me would it be to stay here and be happy while preventing other people from experiencing peace and happiness? And what about what Alistair said? Was I really willing to risk the end, the end of everything, just to be with Jess? I was feeling more emotions than I can describe. It's a surreal feeling to think that you could potentially be responsible for the end of the world. I used to love watching Biblical horror movies like The Seventh Sign and The Omen about End of Days. I remember wondering how I would react if I had a

moral dilemma like that and would I be willing to sacrifice myself for the good of mankind. I guess now I had my answer. Part of me wished that I would wake up and none of this had happened. The flight attendant snapped me out of my thoughts when she offered us cocktails. With how the last hour had gone, she was going to have to keep them coming, but it at least got me out of my head long enough to look at Jess. And as despicable as it may sound looking into her eyes was all I needed to forget about what Alistair had told me, at least for the time being.

The flight attendant gave us a couple of mini bottles of champagne and Jess and I toasted to our Parisian adventure. Jess reached down into her bag and pulled out a travel book on Paris and I could see there were tons of Post-it notes and labels sticking out of everywhere. The entire book had that tattered secondhand bookstore look to it...the sign of an extremely well-read book. It made me think, how many times had she gone through this book? How many times had she flipped through this book alone in her apartment, dreaming of a different life? She clocked my eyes noticing all the labels and she blushed slightly. I pushed those thoughts aside and tried to lighten the mood. "I had no idea you were such a big nerd! Don't get me

wrong, it's cute, I like it!" I could see her nervousness subside and the truth was I did like it, I wasn't lying, but this wasn't Jess. Jess wouldn't have known how to plan anything to save her life. She was always the creative type. She would leave her head at home if it weren't attached to her body. But this Jess, this was a Jess I didn't know everything about. I felt a bit sad that I had missed her change but also a little excited to be honest, that I got to know her all over again.

Jess started flipping through the book and I noticed that nearly every page had something highlighted or underlined on it. She looked up at me. "So, what do you want to do first when we get there?" I smiled. "I figured we would just wander around when we got there." I took the book and started flipping through more pages. It looked like a book belonging to someone who had been to Paris hundreds of times and seen everything the city has to offer, but I knew that wasn't the truth. I cleared my throat and turned to her. "How long have you had this book?" I could tell the question made her feel a little uncomfortable. "I've had it for a long time." I smiled slightly and continued, "Have you always been a planner?" I already knew the answer obviously, but I wanted to see

what she would say. She hesitated for a minute, trying to think of the right way to answer that question. "Not always, but people change." Yes, they do and not always for the better I thought to myself. I was trying not to let the thoughts about my own actions creep into my head because I knew she was on the verge of opening up to me and I wanted to keep pressing her. I downed the last of my champagne and said, "You know, sometimes it's better to not always have a plan just in case it doesn't work out the way you hoped it would." The look on her face changed from one of slight embarrassment to a combination of hurt and anger. "You don't think I know that, you don't think I know that sometimes life doesn't end up the way you planned it? Trust me, I know better than anyone how true that is." Why did I keep sticking my foot in my mouth? I was the one who had planned a life with Jess while she truly lived. I was the one who thought about the future, a future I never got to tell her about and one that was taken away from me. I needed to change the conversation. "You know, it's okay to talk to me about him, I don't think he would mind." She wouldn't even look at me she just stared at the travel book she had taken back from me. "Do you want to know when I got this book?" I nodded. "I got it a few months after Jack died. Back then there were days when I didn't even get out of bed. I used to read this book and daydream about being in Paris with him, walking down the Champs-Élysées, having dinner near the Eiffel Tower, sitting at some smoke-filled café drinking wine surrounded locals. I did that for too long. He was supposed to be my person. We were supposed to have a lifetime of adventures. We were supposed to reminisce about the good old' days when we were old and gray. He wasn't supposed to be gone. I wasn't ready to let him go so I escaped into our own little fantasy." It felt like she had just ripped my heart out. While I was in Heaven, she was stuck in her own personal Hell, and there is nothing I can do to take that pain away from her. It is a part of who she is now. She continued, "Eventually, over time, I was able to at least get up and rejoin the world, but I wasn't the same person anymore." She flipped through some pages in the book. "I used to bring this book with me every year when I went to the cemetery to visit Jack on the anniversary of his death. When I go visit him I make this pasta dish that we were going to have on the day he died, and I have one place setting for me and one for him and I spend the day there talking to him as if he were still alive." She paused for a minute and laughed to herself. "I probably sound crazy, right?" My heart was breaking listening to her story, but she had finally started to let her guard down so as hard as it was to hear, I wanted her to keep going. I took her hands and kissed them gently. "It doesn't sound crazy at all, Jess." She squeezed my hands reassuringly. "Anyway, every year when I went to see him, I would talk to him about our trip to Paris and what it would be like, where we would go. In a weird way, it was comforting and helped me deal with everything. But I never thought I would actually go to Paris, especially with someone who wasn't Jack."

She sniffled softly, doing her best to not shed a tear. When she felt composed enough, she looked over at me. I didn't really know what to say, all I wanted to do was take her in my arms and I don't know, apologize for leaving her. People always talk about the victims in a tragedy; you forget that it is harder on the survivors. For the rest of their life they have to live with the memories and the ghosts of a life lost. But there was one thing I was curious about. "So, over the years, did you settle on a plan for the things you would see together?" She smiled. "I actually did." She flipped to the end of the book and pulled out a folded piece of paper and handed it to me. I

slowly unfolded it and now it was my turn to smile. It was perfect. It hit all the major tourist sites, Eiffel Tower, the Louvre, Notre Dame and the Moulin Rouge but then it got more personal, a visit to Pere Lachaise Cemetery to see the tomb of Oscar Wilde, a stop at Jacques Genin for a little chocolate fix and loads of wine bars and cheese shops scattered around town. Jess and I used to joke that if we ever made it to Paris, we wouldn't bother with all the fancy restaurants we would just live on wine and cheese, it made me smile that she remembered that. Looking at this list it sounded like the perfect weekend and then I had an idea. "What if this is our itinerary, Jess? What if we do all these things this weekend?"

After everything that happened, maybe I would still get to go on the trip Jess had planned for us. Jess, on the other hand, didn't think it was such a great idea and shot it down quickly. "Eric, no, that's weird!" "Why is it weird?" "It just is, we aren't going on a vacation that I planned for my dead fiancé, it's creepy!" To be fair she had a point. But, seeing this list and everything on it, I knew this was the perfect way for her to say goodbye to me, and to that life, to our life. I turned in my chair to face her directly. "Okay, maybe it's a little strange, but hear

me out. I think we should do this for two reasons. First, it looks like a pretty great weekend that you've planned, and I want to experience that with you. And secondly, you planned this itinerary for Jack and he represents your past, a past you are still stuck in and living with every day. Maybe if we do this together it will be a way for you to say goodbye, goodbye to that chapter in your life and goodbye to Jack, so you can move on and have a life and a future with someone new someday. I'm not saying it has to be me, but you deserve to be happy. You deserve to let someone love you. You deserve to live, Jess. Can you honestly tell me that this life you are living is what you want?"

I could tell that I had gotten through to her, whether she wanted to admit it to herself or to me, deep down she knew everything I had said was true. We sat in silence for a couple of minutes, Jess trying to process everything I had just said to her. Slowly she turned towards me. "Well, you put me on the spot, now it's my turn. What do you see in your future?" It wasn't the question I thought she would ask me, and it threw me for a loop. Honestly, I didn't think I had much of a future to look forward to, especially not after the conversation I had just had with Alistair. I

was pretty sure my future would be very unpleasant to say the least. But once those thoughts left my head all I could think about was the future I envisioned for Jess and me, when I was alive. It was a future that I never got to tell her about. Before I died, we had always said that we wanted to live in the city for the rest of our lives and never have children and our life would be just that, ours. We could come home whenever we wanted or leave town at a moment's notice, we would stay young and fun for the rest of our lives. But that was what Jess wanted and I didn't want to ruin our perfect life, so I never said otherwise.

What I really wanted was pretty much the opposite of that, I just wasn't sure Jess was ever ready to hear it. Now I could tell her all the things I never got to before. The flight attendant passed by and I ordered us a couple more mini bottles of champagne. I was suddenly feeling a little bit vulnerable and nervous and I was pretty sure I was starting to blush. I took a swig of my champagne. "Living in the city is just temporary for me. Eventually I would like to settle down with someone, find a place out in the country, and hopefully start a family. I want one of those families that sit around the dinner table every night and talk, not because they have to but because they enjoy being with each other. I guess it might sound cliché, but I don't want a big life. I just want a real one, if that makes sense." Jess curled her arm around mine. "That sounds like a pretty good life to me." She really had changed. I didn't say a word I just smiled and kissed her on the forehead.

Moments like that made me feel like no time had passed at all. She used to snuggle up with me on the couch in the exact same position. Part of me wondered if there was any part of her, however subconscious, that realized the same thing.

We stayed like that for a few minutes and I enjoyed every second of being able to touch her and feel her warmth against my shoulder. I didn't want the moment to end but I did want an answer to my earlier question. "So, what do you think?" I slid her itinerary over towards her. She picked it up and gave it a long look before turning towards me. "Are you sure it won't be weird for you?" I smiled wide. "I can promise you that having this weekend with you won't be weird at all, I think it will be amazing. So, is that a yes?" She just nodded and leaned over and kissed me. "Thank you." I looked deep into her eyes. "Thank you for what?" "I don't even know, for everything, all of it, for this moment, this conversation, for making me come on this

trip." I curled her fingers up into mine. "Jess, I didn't make you do anything, you chose to come with me and I'm very glad that you did." I returned the favor and leaned over and kissed her softly. God how I missed kissing those lips! I could have kissed her all the way to Paris, but she was tired. She snuggled up and went to sleep with her head on my shoulder. I spent the rest of the flight wondering how long I could keep this charade up and how long before the world would see the consequences of what I had done, that is if what Alistair had said to me back in New York was the truth. Only time would tell, I guess. I made a promise to myself then and there that this weekend would be my last on Earth. I would tell Jess the truth. I would return to face the consequences of my actions. I would let the world get back to its regularly scheduled programming. But I wanted one last adventure with Jess. I wanted one last goodbye.

## 26

## JESS

I don't know how I was actually able to sleep considering how excited I was. I was awoken by the beginning of our descent into Charles de Gaulle airport. I rubbed the sleep out of my eyes and looked over towards Eric. He was already awake and had apparently been watching me sleep which was an equal mix of sweet and creepy. Oh God was I snoring? Or drooling? He leaned over and gave me a kiss on the forehead. "Good morning, sunshine. We should be on the ground in about thirty minutes, give or take." He pointed out the window and Paris was slowly coming into view. I don't know what I was expecting to feel but from this high angle Paris just looked like another city. I still couldn't believe I was here. I opened the piece of paper with the itinerary written on it. The page was tattered and worn from being opened so many times over the years. Some of the typed words along the creases had faded over time. I looked at the list of things to do and in that moment a twinge of sadness came over me, but it was brief and confusing. I was so excited to be in Paris but I was also so sad that Jack never got to see it with me. Would he

be okay with me seeing and doing all of these things with someone else? I hope so. I don't know, it all felt so jumbled in my head. One thing

Eric said kept popping into my head: I was still living in the past. I don't want to be a robot anymore. I don't want to just watch life go by. I want to live it!

Once we landed it was surprisingly quick getting out of the airport. We hopped in a taxi and were zipping through the streets of Paris in no time. I couldn't stop smiling as we drove through the city. Everywhere you looked people were sitting at cafes drinking espresso and smoking cigarettes. It was perfect. It was just how I had pictured it for all these years. I looked over at Eric and he wasn't even looking at the scenery he was watching me. It made me blush. He makes me blush. It's been so long since I felt anything close to happiness that I'm not sure how to handle it. It made me feel like an awkward teenager. He took my hand in his and gave it a gentle kiss. I'm so glad I decided to come on this trip with Eric. Our taxi driver took the scenic route through the Arc de Triomphe and I got my first glimpse of the Eiffel Tower. It was magic. Paris is magic. This moment is magic. What was happening to me? I barely knew Eric and yet here I was halfway around the world with my heart nearly bursting out of my chest. It didn't make any sense at all. This wasn't me, well not anymore at least. We pulled up to the Four Seasons Hotel George V. When Jack was alive we had always joked that we would just pick the nicest hotel in the city and say screw it because it was a once in a lifetime trip.

As I got out of the taxi I tried to take in as much as I could. I wanted to savor every second. Even if it was based on a dream from a lifetime long since gone, it would still be the trip of a lifetime. We headed towards check in and the hotel was just stunning. Initially I felt out of place. It was a weird feeling, even though I was an adult this place made me feel like a little kid. I wanted to tiptoe through the place because I was afraid to break something. Also, I was half expecting someone to come up to us and kick us out for not looking classy enough. I looked over at Eric giggling like a little schoolgirl. He asked me what was so funny. I said it was nothing, that I was just happy but that wasn't entirely true. In all honesty, I was thinking about how Jack would be reacting. He would do his best to pretend he was some fancy rich guy who didn't feel out of place and wasn't impressed by the splendor of the hotel. Then he would look at me and turn bright red because

he knew I could always see right through his bullshit. Eric was different. He was more interested in me. He really didn't even seem to notice the opulence of the hotel. We walked up to reception and began to check in and then I had a thought. "Excuse me, by any chance, is the penthouse suite available?"

That got Eric's attention. He leaned in and whispered to me, "What are you doing? Do you know how much that is?" I shushed him right as the receptionist told me that it was indeed available so I asked her how much it cost per night. "Combien ça coûte par nuit?" She smiled and calmly said, "€16,000 par nuit." Before I could speak Eric grabbed my hand and pulled me away from the counter. "What are you doing?" I smiled ear to ear for a second because I saw a little twinge of Jack in his reaction. Jack would have done the same thing, pretend he was okay with the price until he actually thought I might try to book it. The truth was that I could easily afford it. "Eric, look, I wasn't sure I wanted to tell you this, but I don't like secrets. This trip is paid for. I never touched Jack's life insurance so it's just been sitting in an account collecting interest since he died. I'd never wanted to spend it until we decided to come here. Somehow I thought he would approve of

it." Eric didn't say anything at first, he just looked at me silently and then he tried to speak. "Look, I just—" But I cut him off, grabbing his hands. "Eric, this is my money and I will spend it how I want to, okay?" He just nodded yes, and I walked back over to the reception desk and asked to be upgraded to the penthouse. It wasn't until my American Express card cleared that the woman behind the counter smiled back at me.

Walking into the suite was beyond imagination. I felt like Julia Roberts in Pretty Woman, minus the prostitution, of course. The master bathroom was bigger than my apartment in New York! We said goodbye to the bellhop and as he closed the door, I couldn't help myself any longer. I ran through the room squealing. Once I was done, I leaned casually in the doorway between the bedroom and the living room and I looked at Eric. "So, what do you think?" He calmly walked over and put his arms around my waist and kissed me. "I think it's perfect, but you aren't spending another dime on this trip and I don't want to hear any fuss about it." I just nodded yes and kissed him back. He took my hand and led me out onto the private balcony. There was a small table with a bottle of champagne chilling in an ice bucket. It was getting late and the sun was already

beginning to set across the city. I walked over and poured a couple glasses of champagne while Eric put our bags in the bedroom and rejoined me. I wanted to pinch myself. I still couldn't believe I was actually in Paris staring at the Eiffel Tower from the balcony of my hotel room. People dream of a place like this. I know I had.

But there was still that lingering sadness for Jack. I glanced casually up to the sky above the Eiffel Tower and wondered to myself about whether or not Jack was actually up there. And if he was, what would he be thinking right now? Eric walked over towards me. "Penny for your thoughts?" He snapped me out of my daydream, and I looked at him and told him nothing. He picked up the glasses of champagne and handed me one and added, "You're thinking about Jack?" Busted. I turned towards him. "I'm sorry I just have a lot of things flying through my head right now. Yes, I am thinking about Jack but I am also thinking about you and how less than a week ago you were in a coma and all you were to me was a patient." He smirked and inched closer to me. "But I'm something more now?"

How does he do that? He makes my heart skip a beat with just a few words. I stammered, "I don't know...yes...n- no...maybe?" Thankfully he stopped me from turning into a

stuttering mess. He took my hand and we sat down at the table on the balcony. I apologized but I wasn't exactly sure what I was apologizing for. I know he understands so why am I making things more confusing and awkward? He lifted up his glass. "I know you are probably feeling a million different things right now and I don't want you to feel like you can't talk about those things or feel like you need to hide anything from me. I do have one thing to say though." He scooted a little closer to me. "Whatever happens with us I just wanted to say thank you for this weekend." He raised his glass and I met his with mine. "Cheers... to living in the moment." We clinked glasses. "And speaking of living in the moment, I am going to need you to go get changed." I smiled. "Why? Where are we going?" Eric started laughing. "Nice try. It's a surprise so you get your butt in there and put on something nice." I couldn't have hidden my excitement even if I wanted to. I got up from the table and started walking into the bedroom but I turned and walked back over to Eric and kissed him. "Thank you for getting me to come here, it means more to me than I think you even know." He ran his fingers through my hair. "You're welcome, J. Now get moving, we have to be there in an hour." I turned and hustled into the bedroom and a

thought fleetingly crossed my mind. Jack used to call me "J" as a nickname, it was a strange coincidence and it threw me off momentarily but it quickly went out of my mind as I went into the bathroom. I showered quickly and started getting ready for the evening. Thankfully I am not a high maintenance kind of girl, so I was able to do my hair and makeup fairly quickly. I put my hair up since we were going somewhere nice. I can't even remember the last time I took the time to do my hair. Usually I just have it in a ponytail. I came out of the bathroom wrapped in a towel.

Before I'd gotten into the shower, I had laid out a long black dress with spaghetti straps and a pair of black gloves. I wasn't even trying to hide the fact that I ripped off the idea from Breakfast at Tiffany's. I slid on the dress and gloves and gave myself a once over before I walked out of the bedroom.

Eric clearly was trying to impress me because he looked impeccable in a dark blue suit with a small white pocket square sticking out. As soon as he saw me his eyes widened, and a huge smile came across his face. He walked towards me. "You look incredible! So, should I call you Holly for the evening?" I laughed. "Well done, most guys don't know Breakfast at Tiffany's."

"Well, I am not most guys." "I am beginning to see that," I replied. He reached out his hand and I placed mine in his and we walked out of the room towards the elevator.

The whole way down to the lobby and out onto the street we didn't say a word. We just held hands and stared into each other's eyes as we walked. My heart was pounding the entire time. It sounds simple—we were just walking—but it was one of the most romantic few minutes I had ever had. Here was this gorgeous man who could care less about anything around him. All he wanted to do was stare at me. I could feel myself falling more and more for him with every passing second.

I am in trouble.

As we walked down Avenue George V the sun continued to set. This time of day has always been my favorite. As the sun says goodbye it just feels like the world slows down ever so slightly. And today on this street in Paris it was no different. The sounds around the city seemed to be becoming more and more muted with every passing second. We crossed Pont de l'Alma and paused momentarily to watch the boats going up and down the Seine. Every person was in their own little world. No one cared that I was holding hands with someone I was desperately trying to not fall for. No one cared that I was failing miserably at the task either. We were just two additional strangers in a city full of them.

We crossed the bridge and turned right on Quai Branly and there in front of me was the Eiffel Tower in all its glory. I looked at him and spoke for the first time in maybe twenty minutes. "Are we going to the Eiffel Tower?" I asked him. He gave my hand a gentle squeeze. "Something like that." "Well is it something like that or is it that?" He wouldn't budge but the tower kept getting closer and closer. We had to be going there because we walked right to it. I can't believe I was finally getting to see the Eiffel Tower in person after all the years of just looking at it as a picture in an old book. We walked past the queue and I looked at him but again he said nothing. A little further up the esplanade he turned towards another much smaller queue. I looked up at the sign and it said, 58 Tour Eiffel Restaurant. I couldn't contain my excitement. "We are EATING at the Eiffel Tower?!" He looked at me and just smiled. I grabbed his face and kissed him. Then he came back with, "I mean, it's no penthouse suite, but I think I did okay." I think he did more than okay but I'm not going to tell him that. I've already tipped my hand enough and we

have only been in Paris for a few hours. I have to at least attempt to keep some semblance of control over myself but who am I kidding I'm a lost cause already. I just still can't get my head around the fact that I didn't even know Eric a week ago and now I am falling head over heels for him. For the first time in a long time, I felt like me.

Only one other man in my life has ever made me feel the way that Eric has so far, like your once sturdy world is shifting beneath your feet. Jack used to believe soulmates were real and truthfully after Jack passed I just sort of resigned myself to being alone because I had my person and he was taken away from me. But maybe I was wrong. Maybe there is more than one person out there for each of us. I don't want to think about that right now though. Here is this wonderful man who has broken me out of this cocoon that I have been trapped in for so many years. It is not fair to him to be constantly thinking about my past. I do want to live in the moment again. I need to get out of my head and stop thinking. I am minutes from having dinner at the Eiffel Tower; I want to remember every moment of this experience for the rest of my life. Jack has been my life for as long as I can remember but the truth is, he is my past. Eric could be my future. Who knows, maybe he came into

my life to help me say goodbye to Jack and a life that doesn't exist anymore. Either way he deserves me being present. More than that I can feel my heart being drawn to his. I didn't think I would ever feel this feeling again and I want to do everything in my power to make sure it doesn't stop.

## 27

## JACK

I can't believe Jess paid €16,000 for a hotel room! But I'm not going to lie I felt a little better when she said that it was paid for with the money from my life insurance policy. I thought it was a stupid idea and a waste of money for someone in their twenties to have life insurance. I rarely listened to my parents' advice but in that moment, I was glad that I had. In a weird way, it was sort of like we were paying for the trip together, not that I could tell her that or anything. But more importantly, even if it was so slight that she didn't notice, Jess was starting to act like the girl she used to be when I was alive. She would throw caution to the wind more than anyone I knew. It made me smile inside to know that just maybe this whole crazy plan was starting to work. Jess was coming back to life.

    All my thoughts left my head the second she walked out of the bedroom. She was breathtaking. Time slowed as she walked across the room. She looked down at the floor as she moved closer and closer towards me. The click of her heels seemed to be timed perfectly with my pulse. In that moment,

    we were in perfect harmony. We were no longer two separate entities. Her eyes met mine and I felt like she was seeing me, not Eric. She was seeing past the shell; past the horrible choices I had made over the last few days. We were back together in our tiny one-bedroom apartment in the city.

I didn't know what to say, so I didn't say anything. The whole world faded away and it was just us. I remember how we would lie in bed and Jess would talk about all the things she wanted to do in Paris whenever we had the money to go. She definitely wanted to be a tourist but she also wanted to live a little bit like a local. To just stroll down the Seine like it was a normal Tuesday. So that is what we did. We didn't even speak we just held hands and walked. I knew where I was going, but in this moment, I wasn't even thinking about that. All I was thinking about was this beautiful woman, this perfect woman I had loved my entire life—my entire afterlife. The sun was setting, her favorite time of day, and she looked at peace for the first time since I died. She wasn't thinking about how crazy it was to be in Paris with a virtual stranger. She was just experiencing every moment, every second, just like I was. We were the only two people, in our own little world,

nothing else matters. I know I feel exactly the same way I always felt when I was around Jess, but what is she feeling? I am not Jack, in her eyes at least. But maybe deep down somewhere she knows it is me. I can only hope that is the case when it comes time to tell her the truth.

As we walked up to the Eiffel Tower Jess lit up like a Christmas tree. She had fantasized so long about the Eiffel Tower. I was able to book us a table to have dinner at 58 Tour Eiffel. I wasn't sure if it was going to be too touristy for her, but one look at the smile on her face told me that I had made the right choice. Riding up to the restaurant in the elevator I couldn't take my eyes off her. I didn't think it was possible for her to smile so wide.

The elevator stopped at the first floor where the restaurant is and before we got off Jess leaned in and kissed me. "Thank you for this."

The maître d' took us to our table by the window. Jess couldn't stop smiling. A soft candle illuminated the table in an amber glow. And just beyond the glass, the Parisian skyline twinkled. Everything was perfect. Almost perfect.

Off to the side, through another window, I could see the next elevator heading up. While Jess was looking around the restaurant and taking every detail in, I was focused on that elevator and the gray swirling cloud that appeared next to a tall woman, its features were even more defined than before. It had a distinctly human shape to it. I could only see it for a brief moment before the elevator doors clicked shut and it moved up to the next floor. I feared that Alistair was telling the truth. It was getting worse.

"Is everything okay?" I snapped out of my daze at Jess's question. I looked at her briefly then smiled. "Yes, sorry, just zoned out." She looked at me like she wasn't quite sure she believed me. "You look like you've seen a ghost." I was worried she was more right than she realized. The waiter came and took our orders. All I was thinking about was Alistair. If that was indeed a soul it was becoming more solid at least it looked that way to me. He had told me they would eventually become visible to everyone. I had to just hope and pray he was wrong, but let's be honest I don't think anyone up there is going to be listening to or answering my prayers.

Jess got my attention. "Can I ask you something?" I told her of course, she could ask me anything. She took a big sip of her champagne. "What was it like?" "What was what like?" I asked her. She replied, "What was dying like?" It was a question I honestly hadn't considered that she might ask me. She continued, "Was there a white light or I don't know, what do you remember if you remember anything at all?" What do I tell her? I obviously can't tell her the truth; I can't tell her who I am. At least not yet anyway, I wasn't ready for this to end. So, I did the only thing I could do, I lied. "I don't really remember anything. It felt like I was asleep. I was gone one minute and then I was back." Jess looked dejected. I leaned in. "Were you expecting some grand story?" She laughed. "No, I just think there has to be more after this. It can't just end. I mean, don't you believe in an afterlife?"

Of course, I've been there. She continued, "I just believe that when we pass on there is more, more than just this. Otherwise it would be too scary, if there was just nothing. I want to see my family and my friends again one day, I want to see J—" She got quiet, so I jumped in, "Jack. You can say it." She blushed. "I just think people come into your life for a reason. He was a huge part of my life and I do pray that one day I will get to see him again. And if I am being honest, I think you came into my life for a reason too. I think you are here to help me say goodbye to that life. I think you are here to show me it is okay to move on, it is okay to open my heart up to someone new."

And that is when it hit me. She can never know the truth. I know I made a promise to myself to tell her the truth and that it would be my last weekend on Earth. I would keep half of that promise. She doesn't need to know that I am me. I don't have to put her through that pain and confusion. I am just here to help her let go of the past, to let go of me.

I took her hands in mine. "I am very grateful for the time we have. And if I can help you move on then that makes this time even more special. Jess, you are amazing, and you deserve to be told that every day. You deserve someone who makes you feel like you are the only person in the room.

You deserve to be someone's world again. You shouldn't be hiding in your apartment, hiding from the world, hiding from life. You are too amazing for that." Jess took a deep breath. "You know, I've watched a video from our engagement party, over and over, for years." I almost blurted out, "I know!" But thankfully I managed to keep my mouth shut. She continued, "Truth is, he wasn't supposed to be gone, not when we were so young. They never tell you that when you are going to get married. Sure, there is all the till death do us part stuff in your vows, but no one prepares you for what it is like to have that person one day and then not the next. It took every ounce of me to just get out of bed every day and that went on for so long. Slowly you learn to rejoin the world, but you are never going to be the same person again. I wish you would have known me back then; I think you would have liked me."

I did. I loved you.

She pushed some food around on her plate. "I'm sorry to ramble on like this, but if I am being honest, Jack will always be a part of me. He changed who I was. He changed who I was going to be. But you are right. It is time to close that chapter of my life. I think am ready to do that. And I think am ready to do that with you. I can't tell you how much it means to me that we are sitting here at the Eiffel Tower. Thank you for giving me some new memories and replacing some of those terrible ones." As she finished, I could see a tear trickle down her left cheek. I reached up and wiped it away for her. "If I have learned anything it's that you need to live every moment like it might be your last because it just might be." She nodded in agreement. "Do you have any regrets?" I smiled. "I have more regrets than I can admit but right now I have a second chance to make up for some of those mistakes and I am not going to waste it."

I picked up my glass. "To making memories." We clinked glasses. As I took a sip of champagne, we locked eyes and the world fell away. She was as perfect as the day I met her. As perfect as the day I died when I kissed her goodbye for the last time to go to the bodega. I could tell she felt the moment just as I did because she squeezed my hands harder and her eyes wouldn't leave mine. She dropped her eyes briefly and then coyly looked up at me and smirked. "Should we get out of here?" I nodded yes and raised one eyebrow, which made her laugh breaking the sexual tension briefly.

I paid the bill and we got into the elevator back down to the ground. We were maybe a few hundred feet from the tower when it started to rain, gently at first then harder and harder. Tourists hurried in all directions looking for shelter while local Parisians strolled by under their umbrellas. Jess started giggling as the rain fell but we didn't move any faster and we didn't let go of each other's hands. As the rain came down harder, I gave her my jacket. "Should we make a run for it?" She looked at me with water

running down her face. "Nope! This is perfect. I don't want to miss a moment."

Walking back across the Pont de l'Alma with the rain pouring down around us was beautiful and eerie. The heavy rain made ripples in the Seine and added a glossy sheen to the surrounding buildings, nobody on the bridge but us. I was completely soaked, and Jess wasn't doing much better. Her hair had gone flat under the weight of all the water, but her smile wouldn't fade. She had never looked more beautiful. Walking hand in hand it was almost as if ten years of pain and sorrow and heartbreak was being washed away and she was once again that carefree girl who brought me out of my shell all those years ago. She grabbed my hand and we ran the last little part of the bridge, not to get out of the rain but to jump in a puddle that had formed at the end of it. She let out a big laugh as she landed, with both feet, in the puddle.

We finally got back to the hotel and the bellhop looked at us like we were aliens as we calmly walked through the lobby, sopping wet. I waived to him as we passed. "Bon nuit!" We got into the elevator and just stared at each other smiling. She walked over and fixed my hair and kissed me long and slow until the elevator stopped

on our floor. Once inside she took my coat off and shivered slightly. "Do you want me to call down for some tea or something?" She chuckled to herself and walked over to me. She took me by the hand and turned towards the bedroom adding as an afterthought, "No, not even a little bit."

She closed the door behind me and turned to face me. This was a moment I had thought about ever since I died, the fact that I would never be able to be with Jess again. I would never be able to touch her, to hold her, to make love to her again. But here I was in the exact moment I had always wished for and I felt myself hesitating. Was it right to do this? On the one hand, if Jess knew it was me there would be no question, but she didn't. She thought this was the first moment in the beginning of a new relationship. How could I do that to her? But I wanted to be with her so badly it hurt. The other thing I had to consider was how much longer I was even going to be here.

For all I know I could drop dead at any moment and if that happened what would that do to Jess? But I can't bring myself to tell her the truth. She deserves happiness even if it is just for an evening or a moment.

She came closer, so close that I could smell what was left of the perfume she had on. I put my hands on her cheeks and asked her, "Are you sure?" She leaned in and kissed me and that was all the validation I needed. She slowly unbuttoned my shirt and tossed it on the floor near the bed. I turned her around and unzipped her dress and slid the straps delicately from each of her shoulders. Her dress joined my wet shirt in a pile on the floor. I picked her up and she wrapped her legs around my waist as I carried her over to the bed.

My God, she was beautiful. The scene couldn't have been more perfect. The rain continued to pour down outside while in the bedroom we made love for the first time in years, or the first time ever, depending on your perspective.

## 28

## JESS

Waking up this morning I felt like a completely different person. Everything just felt a little brighter. The sky looked bluer. The people walking outside seemed more alive. It's hard to explain it, but for the first time in a long while, I felt like I was actually part of the world and not just someone watching it all happen. And it is because of more than just last night. That is a part of it of course, but that isn't the only reason. It's Eric, it's how he came into my life, it's Paris, it's all of it. I feel alive. I feel happy. I finally feel like myself. I'd forgotten what that felt like.

I rolled over and looked at Eric. He was sleeping peacefully next to me, his chest rising and falling with every breath. Last night was a perfect night if there existed such a thing. From our dusk walk along the Seine to dinner at the Eiffel Tower and the soaking wet walk back to the hotel. I know I had been trying to fight it but there was no point. Eric just got me, he understood me inside and out. We haven't even known each other for that long but it was an unmistakable truth. I felt lucky enough to have felt

it with Jack. But to feel it once more is almost too much. The little voice in my head kept telling me that it can't be real and to prepare myself for the ball to drop. But I ignored her. The whole evening was something out of a fairy tale. I kept waiting to wake up alone in my bed with that all too familiar heaviness in my heart. But I never did.

The way he kissed me, the way he held me, the way he made love to me made me feel like we had known each other for a lifetime. Could I be so lucky as to find another person I had that kind of connection with? Take things slow Jess.

That is what the voice kept telling me. But who am I kidding. This is happening. This is real and I am determined to enjoy every moment of it.

Eric looked at me. His bed head was ridiculous, and he had sleep crusted in the corner of both of his eyes. Even looking like a hot mess, all I wanted to do was kiss him, so I did. As I pulled back, he said, "Soooo, last night was...fun." I giggled and hid behind my pillow. "What do you feel like doing today?" I reached over to the nightstand and grabbed my itinerary, giving it a quick once-over and knew immediately what we should do. I rolled back over so I was next to him and fiddled with his chest hair. "I think we should just go for a walk since it's a nice gloomy Sunday and we can end up at Père Lachaise Cemetery. It's a beautiful old cemetery and—" He cut me off and finished my sentence, "And that is where Oscar Wilde is buried and you want to go and see his tomb." I nodded and replied, "I do." He gave me a kiss and hopped out of bed naked and casually strolled into the bathroom. I could get used to that view.

The second I heard the shower going I wrapped myself in the bed sheets and got up to find my phone; I needed to call Andrea. I wasn't even sure what time it was, but it didn't matter. I finally got a hold of her on the second try. She sounded groggy; clearly, she was still in bed. "Hello," she answered sleepily. I whispered, "Andrea, wake up, it's me. I don't have long to talk. He is in the shower." There was a momentary pause and I could hear her sitting up in bed. "Wait, did you two..." I didn't say anything, but clearly my silence spoke volumes because all Andrea could do was scream into the phone! Breathlessly she said, "Okay, tell me everything! How was it? Was it good? Is he..."?

"Andrea!" She laughed. "What? You know you want to tell me!" Of course, I did, but I wasn't going to. "I'm not telling you that!" "Prude!" I could almost hear her rolling her eyes. "We went on a walk to the Eiffel Tower and he

surprised me with dinner there too! When we were walking home afterward it started pouring rain and when we got back to the hotel we made—" Andrea jumped in, "Are you about to say that you made love? Jess, are you falling in love with him?" I think I was. I think I am falling in love with him.

I was lost in my thoughts when I heard the bathroom door start to open. "Andrea, I have to go, love you, bye!" I had just managed to hang up the phone when Eric came out of the bathroom. He had a towel wrapped around his waist and water dripping down his shoulders and chest. As he dried it, he asked me, "Were you talking to someone?" I did my best innocent impression. "Me? No. I'm going to get in the shower if you're all done in there." I climbed out of bed and gave him a kiss before heading into the bathroom.

It was a pretty chilly day and we grabbed a few coffees before we walked into the cemetery. I don't know what it is about cemeteries, especially old ones but they are beautiful. There is an eerie peacefulness in the air. There were no sounds but the wind rustling and a few birds in the distance. It was fairly empty. Lining both sides of the walkway are tombs, headstones, and mausoleums, some as old as the twelfth century.

I'd read in my travel book that the oldest known grave in the cemetery belongs to Peter Abelard, a theologian and poet, who died in 1142. He was buried along with his wife Heloise. They had a pretty tragic love affair. Abelard was hired by Heloise's uncle to be her tutor. But life had other plans. They fell in love, married and eventually had a child together. Her family was outraged and had Abelard castrated. After that he became a monk and Heloise ended up joining a convent. As awful as that story is, they found each other again, in death. I know it's morbid but there is something beautiful about where they ended up. They will spend eternity side-by-side. I had a similar plan for myself. When it was my time, I would be buried next to Jack, so we could be together again.

We would go several minutes before crossing paths with another person. It took a little wandering around, but we finally found the tomb of Oscar Wilde. It stood out among the more traditional tombs as it was shaped like a Sphynx. Seeing the tomb made me smile. Oscar Wilde always made me think about the good times with Jack. But the longer I was here with Eric the more it really did feel like it was time to close that door. I was finally getting closure, something I know Jack would have wanted for me. Eric too

was smiling, probably because he knew he was getting major brownie points by coming here with me. I walked up to him and put my hand on the small of his back. "Do you know what one of the last things Oscar Wilde said before he died was?" Eric said he didn't. "He was in his house and he knew his time was short. He said, 'Either this wallpaper goes, or I do.'" Eric laughed and added, "So I guess the wallpaper stayed. Why did you and Jack like Oscar Wilde so much?" I replied, "Well, it was actually Jack who got me into him. Oscar Wilde was the ultimate outcast in his time and that was something Jack liked about me back when we were in school. I was a bit of an outsider." I couldn't help but laugh. "I was such a cliché, I tried to rebel against my parents by going through a Goth phase. I looked ridiculous." I walked closer to the tomb and looked at the epitaph and read it aloud:

"And alien tears will fill for him, Pity's long-broken urn
   For his mourners will be outcast men, And outcasts always mourn."

I turned to Eric. "That was from a poem he wrote called The Ballad of Reading Gaol while he was in prison for being a homosexual, which was illegal at the time."

Eric put his arm around me and pulled me closer and I continued, "And do you see all the lipstick kisses?"

Scholars attribute that to a line from A Woman of No Importance, which said that 'A kiss may ruin a human life.' And that is also why there is the glass barricade now because all the lipstick kisses were ruining the tomb." Ugh, shut up, Jess! Why was I babbling so much? I'm pretty sure Eric didn't give a damn about what the quotes on Oscar Wilde's tomb meant, let alone any of the other information I was spewing out at an ever-increasing speed. I turned from the tomb and looked at Eric. "I'm sorry for the history lesson." Eric's smile turned into a big grin. "Maybe it's because I make you nervous?" I rolled my eyes at him playfully. "Hardly." He continued, "Are you sure? I can be quite charming when I want to be. I mean, I'm not even really trying and you are basically putty in my hands." He took a few steps backward but he never broke eye contact with me. I took a few steps towards him. "Is that right? Well, let's see what you've got, Casanova! Give me your best shot." Almost immediately his demeanor changed.

His smile faded and his eyes became laser focused on me. Man, this guy had some bedroom eyes! Instinctively I took a step back, but it didn't matter. He took three steps

towards me and had grabbed me around the waist. Before I realized what was happening, he leaned in and planted the softest most sensual kiss I had felt in probably my entire life. And as he pulled away, he whispered, "By the way, the history lesson was adorable." He turned and started walking away but not before grabbing my hand and bringing me along for the ride. He was good.

We walked to the end of the row and turned onto the main pathway through the cemetery. As soon as I came around the corner, we saw a funeral procession in progress.

Everyone was dressed in black walking in silence. At the very back of the procession was an elderly woman walking by herself alongside a coffin being carried by several men.

Eric had stopped walking out of respect, and I came up alongside him to watch them go by. It was beautiful in an incredibly sad way. I looked over at Eric and the expression on his face took me completely by surprise. He looked terrified.

## 29

## JACK

I was enjoying flirting with Jess so much and it was amazing to finally get to see Oscar Wilde's tomb. But my joy was short lived. The funeral procession coming towards us was pretty typical—sad, but typical. Then as it came into closer view, I stopped dead in my tracks. At the back was an elderly woman with a black veil covering her face. She walked with her head down alongside the coffin. That isn't what terrified me, it was what was walking alongside her. As it passed, he looked towards me, HE. It was no longer some swirling form. This had a shape. It had a body. It had a face! It was an elderly man who looked to be the same age as the woman in the veil. All I could assume was that it was the soul of the man IN the coffin.

Any doubt about what was happening disappeared in that moment. Alistair was right. The horror of what I had done came into full focus.

There is one way to stop it, but I wasn't ready to leave her yet. Maybe there was a way to make things right and stay with Jess. I don't want to have to say goodbye to her. I don't want her to be alone again. I had let this go

on too far; I just wanted her to realize there was life beyond me. But now she has fallen for me all over again, I can feel it. How can I end things now? How can I tell her the truth? I fear that if she has to go through the pain of losing someone again, she won't recover. She will be broken, forever. But how can I keep this going when the world around me is falling apart? How much longer can I be selfish like this? I'm trapped. No matter what I do, I am going to hurt her.

I was less than a foot away from Jess, but I might as well have been a million miles away. She could tell by the look in my eyes. She shook my arm. "Eric. What's wrong?" How do I even begin to answer that? Oh, I'm fine, Jess. And by the way, I'm not Eric, I'm your long-dead fiancé wearing an Eric suit! How have you been? Until I felt sure that Jess would be okay or until something stopped me, I would continue to lie. I looked at her. "Sorry, just got a little freaked out, must be because it's an old cemetery or something. I've got a case of the willies." I tried to laugh it off, but I wasn't sure she believed me. I can't keep lying like this to her. It is getting harder and harder. I had to start thinking of a way to get out of this or make things right, I just don't know what the solution

is right now. She took my hand in hers. "Okay, well how about we get out of here and check out the rest of the city?" She leaned in and gave me a kiss and we walked hand in hand out of the cemetery, away from the elderly man who stood by his wife.

We walked in silence for a while. I felt heartbroken and defeated. Everything up until now on this trip has been perfect, too perfect apparently. I needed to snap out of it and enjoy whatever time I had left with Jess; she at least deserved that before her world came crumbling down…again. I tried my best to shake it off. "How about we sit down somewhere and have a coffee." She agreed and we sat down at a little café. We were surrounded by tourists and locals just going about their day. I was envious of them. They had no idea just how close to the end they truly were.

The waiter came over, Jess ordered an espresso and I ordered a glass of wine. Thankfully the waiter spoke English because I was not in the mood to attempt to order in French, I had too much else on my mind. While we waited for our drinks to show up it was clear that Jess could tell something was wrong with me. "So, do you want to talk about what happened back there at the cemetery?" I barely heard what she had to say, I was becoming more and more consumed

with how I was going to tell Jess the truth. How do you even start a conversation like that? It's not like this would be a simple lie to undo, I mean how is she going to react when she finds out that there is an afterlife.

It's such a clichéd saying that you shouldn't take anything for granted, especially life, because you never know when it is going to end. But it couldn't be truer. To feel the wind blowing on your face, to feel the sun shining on your skin, to be able to look into the eyes of the one you love and have them look back into yours, is priceless. We take these things for granted but trust me when your number is up it is all you will be able to think about.

What if I could just have one more hour, one more day, then I would be ready.

I looked up at Jess and came out of my thoughts. She looked concerned. "Eric, ever since the cemetery you have been somewhere else. Did something happen? Did I do something?" I could hear the twinge of fear in her voice. She was internalizing my distance. I took her hands. "No, Jess, it's not about you—" She cut me off, "You were fine one minute and then the next you were just gone." I wanted to just blurt out the truth right there and I almost did. But not yet, I needed her to be in the right headspace if I

had any hope of not ripping her heart out. I looked down at the table briefly to think about what I was going to tell her. I took a deep breath, "I'm sorry, Jess, when that funeral procession went by, it just made me think about my own death."

Technically, I wasn't lying. The best lies are the ones that have some truth to them. I was scaring myself at how good I was becoming at lying. Lies just end up hurting people and I have been doing nothing but lie to the one person I least wanted to hurt in the world. She frowned slightly. "I'm sorry, Eric, I didn't even think about how you might feel a little weird going to a cemetery considering everything you have been through." I shook my head. "No, no, Jess, there is no reason for you to apologize. I'm fine, I promise. It just caught me off guard a little I guess." Her frown turned into more of a concerned look. "Well, how are you feeling now?" I smiled. "I'm good, I promise." Jess was about to say something else when the waiter came towards us holding a tray with our drinks. Just as he got to our table all the color drained from his face. The tray he had been holding tipped out of his hand sending our drinks flying. The red wine sloshed between us and spilled over the side of the table creating a crimson waterfall that ended with a splash on the concrete. The glasses crashed to the floor and shattered into a thousand pieces. Patrons and pedestrians stopped all around to look at the commotion the waiter had caused. The waiter just stood there staring at the same spot. I turned around behind me to look, but there was nothing there. I turned back to him. "Ça va, monsieur?" He didn't respond. I tried again in English, "Sir, are you okay?" His head didn't move but he whispered, "I saw my mother."

Jess didn't seem to be listening to the waiter. She was trying to clean up the mess that was all over the table and her shirt. I walked closer to him. He was now mumbling to himself so softly that I couldn't understand what he was saying. Finally, I got his attention and he repeated, "I saw my mother...I saw my mother." He turned his head from me back to where he had been looking and said softly, "She died a week ago...she died."

I whipped around and followed his gaze in a panic; there was nothing there. But he had seen something, he wouldn't be in this state unless he had. As I stared at nothing, one thought kept recurring in my head.

The end has begun.

## 30

## JESS

I'm starting to worry about Eric. There have been studies on the aftereffects of near-death experiences, but every case is different. I was trying my best to not overthink things, but I am starting to get concerned. As soon as we turned the corner and he saw the funeral procession it was like he had seen a ghost. I mean I get it funerals are hard, trust me I know. I could barely keep it together at Jack's funeral. But Eric was freaking out over a complete stranger. He had never spoken to this woman nor was he ever likely to. Maybe he was just an empathetic person, but I don't know, something just felt off. His explanation did make sense, that it made him think about his own mortality which he had just came face to face with, but if I'm being honest there is a part of me that isn't totally buying it. He didn't seem to want to talk about it and though I wanted to get to the bottom of what was happening I didn't want to push him. This trip has been perfect up until now and I don't want that to change. I never thought I would feel this way about someone again.

So, if Eric needs some time to snap out of whatever is
going on in his head then I am going to give him that time. He deserves that and I deserve this.

## JESS

Leaving the cemetery, I felt like I was doing the right thing by not pushing him to talk. But as the minutes passed and nothing was spoken, I wasn't so sure I had made the right decision. Each minute felt like an eternity. All I wanted to do was help him but did he even want my help? But these thoughts went out of my head the second the waiter dropped our drinks on the table. I looked up at the waiter and he had the same far off look in his eyes that Eric had earlier at the cemetery. When Eric asked him what was wrong, his reply made no sense. He said that he saw what he described as his mother who had passed away over a week ago. I looked at Eric ready to smirk at this crazy guy but Eric was staring at him intently with what I can only describe as a look of pure terror. Why would that scare him so deeply and so quickly? Did he really believe what the waiter said? I looked over Eric's shoulder and there was nothing there. Eric whipped around in his chair and looked in the same direction and didn't see anything either, but I could tell by the look in his eyes he expected to see something. What was happening? I mean this guy is basically saying that he just saw a ghost or something and Eric is

looking at him like he is completely sane. What am I supposed to do with that? I don't believe in ghosts or spirits. If they were real someone by now would have proof of it. I wanted to say something to Eric but what could I say that wouldn't come across as completely condescending, so I didn't say anything. But it made me realize that while my heart was drawn to Eric, I really didn't know him all that well.

This isn't how I thought the rest of this trip was going to go. For feeling like I had known someone my entire life it was like I was looking at a stranger. Eric tried to play it off like it was nothing, but I know what I saw.

Even if it was just for a brief moment, he believed the waiter.

Is this just a one-time thing because of what happened when we were at the cemetery earlier? Or is this who he is? Or maybe it's to do with nearly dying and coming back.

Maybe he did see something, and he just doesn't want to talk to me about it or just isn't ready to talk to me about it because he thinks it might freak me out? If that is the case this isn't helping me to not feel a little freaked out. I need to just put my own feelings aside for now and try and understand him and what he is feeling.

The waiter turned and walked back inside. Eric just sat there in a daze. I reached out and put my hand on his shoulder startling him. He jumped and turned back around to me. I tried my best to smile. "Hey, are you all right?" He looked at me but didn't return the gesture. His eyes were looking at me, but he couldn't have been further away. He sighed. "Yeah, sorry, I'm fine, he just seemed so sure it took me by surprise. Do you want to get out of here?" That was it? That was his explanation? I wanted to ask him so many questions, but I didn't get the chance. I just got up from the table without saying a word. What was I supposed to say? Oh, wait, one quick question, are you crazy by any chance?

We walked back to the hotel in silence or it might as well have been silence because we were basically talking about the weather. We talked about anything and everything except what exactly happened back at the café. Had I felt this all wrong? I couldn't have, dinner at the Eiffel Tower and spending the night together was magic. That was real. I know it was. But now I just felt shut out completely. We went to bed putting on the same airs and pleasantries. The passion we had the night before was replaced with awkwardness.

It was no different in the morning. The closeness I had felt the last few days between us was gone. It felt more like we were just two friends traveling together rather than the beginning of something new and amazing. He kissed me good morning, the excitement from the other night missing. I'm so confused. One day I am riding high and the next the sadness I had felt for the last eight years comes flooding back. It didn't make any sense. I needed to talk to someone about it. While he was in the other room packing, I texted Andrea to make plans to get together, when I get back in town. Hopefully she could help me figure things out.

I finished up packing and we left the hotel for the airport to fly home to New York. I barely slept last night so I just zoned out watching the Parisian streets whiz by. Part of me just wanted to grab Eric and shake him and ask him what the hell his problem was. But I didn't. We sat there, two pleasant "friends" heading home from vacation. Once we were on the plane at least I had movies to distract me from the million thoughts running through my head on a loop. Eric on the other hand seemed completely unphased by the fact that there was basically an ocean between us. What I really wanted to do was ask the flight attendant for the biggest glass of wine she could find and to keep them coming. As amazing as that sounds, I know myself and that would just lead to me to blurting out everything I wanted Eric to know I was thinking and feeling. I just hoped that Eric was taking this time to figure out what he wanted. If he didn't want me fine, just be man enough to tell me and don't drag it out any longer than need be. I think there is something really special here. If he feels the same way he needs to put in the effort and try to help me understand what he is thinking or feeling, whatever it is.

We landed at JFK in the early afternoon. All I wanted right now was to be back in my bed. I was tired of feeling uncomfortable. I was tired of him not telling me what happened. I was just tired. As we got our bags, he looked over at me. "Do you want to share a cab?" No, I don't want to share a cab! I want the guy I have fallen for to realize that he needs to get his head out of his ass and just talk to me. What is happening?

The night we made love as we both drifted off to sleep, I pictured what a future would be like with Eric. I saw us coming home from this trip and joking about whose place we were going to go to from the airport. I saw us holding hands in the taxi ride to my place. And then I saw

what we would be like as a couple. I saw him moving into my place. I saw us bickering about the things of his that I wanted to get rid of. I saw us making dinner. I saw us walking through Central Park in the summer. I saw what a life could be like with Eric. Now I'm just angry. Okay maybe not angry. I'm feeling heartbroken. I just need to be by myself right now to figure some things out and I think Eric needs to do the same. I'm not the kind of girl who forces an issue, but I also just can't be silent. I hope Eric is the kind of man who will come talk to me about his feelings once he figures them out. If not then maybe I was wrong and this isn't anything more than the guy who helps me finally let go of Jack.

My bag came around on the carousel. Eric was still waiting for his bag. I didn't want him to come over, but I didn't want to just leave without giving some explanation however vague it might be. I wheeled my bag over to him. "So, I think I am just going to head home by myself if that is okay with you." He was about to speak but I continued, "Look, I'm not sure what's going on, but something happened with you back at the café. Since then you've been different, and I'm not sure if it has something to do with me or not because you won't really talk about it. Maybe you

need to figure out what you want." He looked flustered. "Jess—" I cut him off again and leaned in and kissed him on the cheek, doing my best to smile when I pulled back. I wet my lips. "I'm going to go. Take some time, figure out whatever it is you need to figure out, and if you decide that you want this then you know where to find me." I turned and walked away before he had a chance to say anything. All I wanted to do as I left the airport was turn back to see if he was watching me walk away like one of those cheesy romantic comedies, but I didn't. This isn't a movie. This is real life and I'm not willing to risk falling even further for someone who isn't sure what he wants. And he has every right to take some time, but I have every right to hold out for everything I deserve.

I got home from the airport and when I walked back into my apartment it had that same empty feeling it always did. It felt like I was being hugged by a blanket of sadness. I sat down on the couch exhaustedly. All I wanted to do was curl up into a ball and put on the most depressing movie I could think of and eat my bodyweight in Ben N' Jerry's ice cream. I resisted the urge to hibernate and text Andrea to confirm plans for later. If anyone was going to help me figure out what happened with Eric it was

going to be her. And if nothing else comes of it I thoroughly planned on drinking myself into oblivion.

Walking to the restaurant later that night I was thinking about exactly what I was going to tell Andrea. Obviously, I would tell her all the good things that happened while we were there but what was I going to say about what happened at the cemetery and then at the café? Should I just be completely honest, or should I filter what I say? I mean if things with Eric and I do work out I don't want to bad-mouth him because that would just make things awkward around my friends. In truth, I was more confused than anything else so I decided that I would just fill her in on everything that happened and see her reaction. I walked into Javier's, my favorite Mexican restaurant, and grabbed a table near the window. While I waited, I ordered a margarita roughly the size of my head. I was halfway through when Andrea barreled into the bar. "I'm so sorry! I couldn't catch a cab and then we got stuck in traffic! I see you started without me, how rude!" On cue the waiter brought over a similarly mammoth-sized margarita for Andrea. She clapped giddily. "And this is why I love you!" She gave me a hug and welcomed me back to town. Once she got comfortable and after she chugged a quarter of her margarita to catch up, she said, "Okay, tell me everything and leave no details out!"

I filled her in on splurging to rent the penthouse suite at the George V and about how Eric surprised me with dinner at the Eiffel Tower and of course I gave her all the sordid details about what came after dinner. I finished my margarita and ordered another round for the both of us. I told her about going to see Oscar Wilde's tomb and how that was something Jack had always wanted to do so it was amazing to finally see it in person. While I was finishing telling her about all that, our next round of margaritas arrived. I took a big healthy chug before I started talking about what came next. I really didn't want to talk about it but thankfully the nearly half a bottle of tequila I had probably just drank had helped with my nerves. I was hesitating and Andrea could tell something was bothering me. "So did something bad happen while you were there? So far everything sounds amazing, but you don't really drink like this, not unless something is wrong." She knew me way too well.

I took a deep breath, and told her everything, from Eric freaking out at the cemetery to what happened with the waiter. I told her all of it, every detail. I held nothing back.

Andrea's eyes bugged out slightly and she let out a big sigh. "So, he is crazy! I knew he was too good to be true." I rolled my eyes. "Andrea, he isn't crazy. At least I hope he isn't. I mean maybe he is some weirdo conspiracy guy who thinks ghosts are real or something like that. But the thing is, he doesn't seem crazy. I mean, maybe nearly dying changes you, I don't know. Now I sound like a crazy person. I just don't get it, up until that point everything was perfect. I hadn't felt anything even close to that since…" Andrea took my hand. "Since Jack?" I nodded and without even realizing it I started to tear up. Andrea got up from the table and came around and hugged me tightly. "Honey, I'm sorry but maybe this is what it is. You had a great trip, for the most part, and now you are ready to get back on the horse or the wagon, one of them anyway. No one is going to be Jack and maybe it's time to move on and let him go." That stung more than I thought it would. She was right though, annoyingly she was often right. I wiped a tear from my eye and took a deep breath. "Maybe you're right but there was, is, just something about him. I mean Andrea, up until this happened, being in Paris with him was

perfect. I felt like he really saw me, in a way only Jack had ever. I just don't understand how it changed so quickly. I just feel like he isn't being honest. He has a secret that he doesn't want to tell me. I'd rather just know the truth, so I don't have to wonder." Andrea went back over to her seat. "Maybe it isn't a weird secret?

Maybe he has a wife or something?" This annoyed me. "What? Why would you think he has a wife?" She shrugged. "I don't know, I mean wouldn't it be better than him believing in ghosts or something? Have you talked to him at all since you got back?" I told her no. She picked up her drink, nearly dropping it. "Well, until you hear from him, I say fuck him! He owes you an explanation or an apology at the very least. And until then I say we drink!" She clinked her glass with mine. I wanted to just say fuck it too, but I can't, I need to know the truth, I need to understand what happened. I need to talk to Eric if for no other reason than to have closure if it really isn't going to go anywhere. But I was going to take Andrea's advice and wait until Eric came to me.

# 31

# JACK

Watching her walk away from me at baggage claim was agony. I just wanted to yell to her "It's me! Jack!" But I just watched the electric doors whoosh open and then close behind her. I saw her silhouette for a few more seconds before she was gone for good. Why did I let her just walk away like that? Why didn't or why couldn't I tell her the truth? Things are only getting worse. I need to come clean with her or figure out how to make things right before she sees the truth with her own eyes. The hard reality is that no matter what I do now Jess is going to be hurt. But isn't it my responsibility to mitigate the damage? When did I become such a coward? I'm letting her walk blindly into danger and I am doing nothing to warn her or protect her.

It felt like an eternity waiting for my bag to come down the conveyer belt. I was in a complete daze trying to figure out exactly how I was going to get myself out of this mess. You know that saying that love makes you do stupid things. Well I am living, or nearly living proof of that. I pretty much gave a middle finger to God to come back here and no matter how clever I thought that I was, I

was going to end up paying a price for that. And I think the punishment is going to be more than a little slap on the wrist. I felt lost and scared and a thousand other emotions that I couldn't put into words. I mean God, GOD is pissed off at me, that'll ruin your Tuesday. Cracking jokes is my defense mechanism, but the truth is I'm terrified, I can't see a way that this doesn't end really horribly.

Either Jess hates me for eternity or God does, or both! Things are pretty bleak right now, I'm not going to lie.

Heading back to Eric's place I just felt numb. I just stared blankly out the window. The New York City streets were teeming with pedestrians moving about their day. It felt like they and I were moving in slow motion. Mixed within the crowds were several souls. They stood out because they were not moving with the masses but rather just standing there. No one seemed to react to them but how much longer until what happened in Paris, happens here? How long before all of this came crashing down? Days? Hours?

Minutes? I paid the taxi driver and walked into Eric's building. Once I got inside, I plopped down on the couch exhausted. I needed to figure out what to do, I couldn't wait any longer. The only problem is that it is such an overwhelming problem that I didn't even know where to start

so I turned on the television. I just needed to turn my brain off for a few minutes. But unfortunately for me a break from all this was not in the cards. On the tv, a local reporter was talking to a woman about storm damage to her house. She was in her mid-forties with messy salt and pepper hair. The reporter and the woman were both standing in front of what must have been her house. I say must have been because, the front porch was now covered by a tree that had fallen during the storm. The woman who was identified as Eleanor Reyes by a chyron, was telling the reporter about the storm and her husband Hector who had died of a heart attack as a result of the tree crashing almost into his living room. She was clearly fighting back tears telling the reporter about her husband of nearly twenty years and what a kind and generous man he had been in life.

The reporter's name popped up on the screen, it was Caroline Morgan. She was coiffed to the nines, with her severely blonde hair pulled back in an immaculate bun.

After expressing her condolences to Eleanor, though I'm not sure there was much in the way of actual compassion, but feigned compassion nonetheless; Caroline asked a question that got my attention. She asked Eleanor, "I'd like to discuss what you told our news director yesterday about what you saw." Eleanor cleared her throat and spoke, "Well, it was about four hours after the storm had passed and the paramedics had just pulled away with Hector's body. I didn't know what to do with myself, I still don't, but I turned around to look at the house and there he was, standing in front of the tree, my Hector." Tears filled her eyes and she pointed to the spot where she said she saw Hector. Caroline after a moment of consoling, or a dramatic pause for effect, continued, "So, Eleanor, let me get this straight, the coroner had just left with your husband's remains and yet you say that you saw him standing in front of the house?" Eleanor nodded in agreement. "I know how it sounds but I'm telling the truth, I believe it was Hector's spirit saying goodbye to me. It was the most beautiful thing. Seeing him one last time made me feel better, it made me feel at peace. And after a moment he vanished." Caroline thanked Eleanor for speaking with her and sharing her story then she turned and walked away from Eleanor towards the camera. When she was out of Eleanor's earshot she spoke directly to the camera, "So what really happened here? Did Eleanor Reyes really receive a message from beyond the grave or was it merely a case of a grieving widow seeing what she wanted to see, one last time? I'll leave that for you to decide, this is Caroline Morgan reporting from Flushing Meadows."

I clicked off the television. The remote felt like it weighed 500lbs in my hand. I slowly let it drop onto the couch. Caroline's words replayed in my head 'merely a case of a grieving widow seeing what she wanted to see'; If only that were true. Things are about to explode if the news is already picking up stories of people seeing their loved ones after they have passed. How long before someone gets a picture of their deceased loved one? I thought about the fear and the pain those who have lost someone would feel.

And the helplessness of knowing there is nothing they can do to fix it. And then it hit me. I know who I need to speak to first about all this before the truth comes out. If I am going to make this right I need to start at the beginning. I need to speak to Eric's parents and come clean. They deserve to know the truth. They deserve to hear it from me before it is too late. They deserve to know what happened to their son.

I knew they were planning on staying in the city for a while, so I called them at their hotel and told them I wanted to see them and tell them about my trip to Paris with Jess. Obviously, I didn't say anything about what I really wanted to talk to them about: "Hey, not Mom and Dad, can I come over and tell you all about how I stole your son's body? Great, see you in an hour!" I mean come on, I know that I am not the best person in the world, especially after all I have done up until this point, but I am not completely heartless. I hopped on the subway and made it to midtown pretty quickly. When I got to their hotel I stopped outside. I just needed a minute to collect my thoughts because once I did this there was no turning back. I mean for all I know this is what sends me back to Heaven or most likely Hell. I looked up towards Times Square and the number of souls had grown into the hundreds. It would soon reach a tipping point. I needed to hurry. I can't leave all these people in pain, in limbo, anymore. And that was just here. If what Alistair said was true, this is happening all over the world. People all over the world were about to find out that their loved ones have not crossed over and if something happens to them, they won't cross over either. I am not going to be responsible for the end of existence, no matter how much I want to be with Jess. It's time to end this. Eric's parents deserve to hear the truth and I just hope I have enough time to speak to Jess, if she will even speak to me. I want her to know the truth. I want her to know that I am me. I want to be able to say goodbye to her because I will never see her again, in this life or the next. The idea to leave and just not tell anyone wasn't going to work. I was brave enough to defy God, I needed to be equally brave, to make things right. Consequences be damned.

The elevator dinged as we passed each floor. The silence between the dings seemed to grow longer and longer. Maybe the elevator could sense how nervous I was or maybe it knew somehow just how badly this was going to go so it was taking its time; eventually the elevator stopped, and the doors opened when I reached the tenth floor. I tried to keep my breathing steady as I knocked on the door. I was hoping I would be able to ease into the conversation somehow. The door opened and Betty came flying in for a hug with a squeal. Bob wasn't far behind. Why did they have to be so nice? Why couldn't they be assholes? That would make all of what was about to happen so much easier for me. But I guess that is part of the point. I had done something horrible, something unspeakable and it was time for my penance. I had to destroy two of the nicest people I had ever met in my life, or afterlife. I did my best to hug them back, but it must have been half-hearted because Betty immediately wanted to know what was wrong. I walked over and sat down at the little table in the corner of their hotel room. I could barely look them in the eye. It's easy to lie to ourselves about the horrible things we do in our lives, but that can only last for so long. Eventually our lies catch up with us. The chickens come home to roost.

Pick your phrase. Here I was, the mirror was turned on me. I was staring at myself and what I had become. I was a monster. I am Dorian Gray.

Betty sat at the table across from me and Bob came over and stood behind her. She took my hand in hers. "What is wrong, honey? Are you feeling okay?" I pulled my hand back from hers. I'd always known this was going to be hard, but it was so much harder than I could have possibly imagined. I was about to destroy this woman. She believed that because of her faith she had her son back and I am about to tell her it was all a lie. All her faith, her belief in God, was for nothing. Her son was gone. That alone was more than I think most people would be able to handle but then I had to somehow make her understand that because of what I did Eric hasn't crossed over yet, that he is stuck in limbo. What were they going to do when they found out that I had violated not only their trust but also their faith and their son?

I took a deep breath. "Can you both sit down? I need to tell you something." Betty instantly looked worried. Bob I think was more curious than anything else. Betty tried to take my hands again, but I pulled them away from her before she had the chance. "Eric, you are acting very strange, did something happen in Paris?" I shook my head. "No. I mean, well, it happened before Paris. And please don't call me Eric." Betty sat back in her chair. "Why wouldn't I call you Eric, honey?" I squeezed my eyes shut and took a deep breath and tried to speak the words, but they wouldn't come out. Betty looked over at Bob with a mix of concern and confusion. Bob piped up, "Eric, you are scaring your mother, what do you need to tell us?" I got up from the table. I couldn't look them in the eye anymore. I couldn't handle watching the hope drain out of their eyes. I paced around the room for what felt like several minutes but probably was more like a few seconds. "Eric, you need to start talking! What is going on?" Bob had clearly had it with my waffling. I turned around and just stared at them. I didn't say a word. "ERIC!" And then I just blurted it out. "MY NAME IS NOT ERIC!"

The words hung in the air like a heavy cloud. I don't think any of us knew what to say for a few minutes so we just all stood there in awkward silence. I spoke first. "My name is Jack, I am a Guardian Angel and I took possession of your son's body at the moment...at the moment he crossed over." Betty gasped and I'll be damned if Bob didn't start laughing but it wasn't a genuine laugh, he clearly thought what I was saying was ridiculous. He took a step out from behind Betty. "Is this some kind of joke, Eric? Because it isn't funny." His smile faded. I took a step closer to them. "It's not a joke, Bob. When I was alive my name was Jack." Now it was Betty's turn to smile, but her smile was genuine. This was not going how I thought it was going to go. She got up and walked over to me and just stared for a moment. "So it's all real? Heaven, Angels, God, it's all real." I nodded yes. She was missing the most important part of the story, that her son was gone. Why?

Betty hugged me. I let her. The truth is I wanted her to let me off the hook. But then I pulled away. "Please don't hug me, there is more and when I am finished, I think hugging me is the last thing you are going to want to do." It was time to rip off the Band-Aid.

I led Betty back over to the table and sat her down.

She deserved to know everything. They both did. There is no turning back now. She asked me how it all started. This time it was my turn to take her hands. "It all started with a girl named Jess Miller. When I was alive, she was my fiancée, she was my world. She was my soulmate." I told them our story, how we had met, how we had fallen in love, and then I told them about how I died. I told them about my experiences in Heaven. The words just came pouring out of me faster than I was able to control them. I paused briefly to collect my thoughts. Betty and Bob both looked completely overwhelmed. I was pretty sure they hadn't even begun to process what I was saying. They looked more like children listening to their parents tell them a bedtime story. I continued, "I needed to be able to help Jess. I needed to help her move on, but she couldn't see me. I needed to figure out a way to come back to her. When I died, Jess died, and I needed to find a way to help her learn how to live again. And that is how Eric came into the equation." That is when a flip switched in Bob. He got up from his chair, rage on his face. "Betty, come on, you are not buying this, are you? Eric, I don't know what has come over you but enough is enough!" He started coming towards me, but Betty interjected, "BOB! GO FOR A WALK...NOW!" We both froze. He turned back to look at Betty. "Betty, please tell me you aren't—" She cut him off, "I said go for a walk now!" The anger in her eyes was palpable. I didn't think there was a side like this to Betty she seemed like such a soft-spoken grandma type. I guess don't judge a book by its cover. I'm living proof of that. Bob didn't say another word he calmly picked up his coat and walked out. The door slamming snapped me out of my daze. I looked at Betty. "Why do you believe me so easily?" She smiled sweetly and gestured to the chair for me to sit down. "Because, I have faith." Maybe I was wrong about much more than I realized. Faith, true faith, can be a powerful thing.

We sat back down at the table and she looked at me sweetly. "Now please, Jack, tell me the rest of your story." I told her about my plan to come back and help Jess. I told her about my plan to "borrow" someone the moment they were to cross over. I told her about finding Eric's file in the Office of Human Resources. She sat there calmly listening, I couldn't tell if she was upset or not, she just listened. Then I told her about the moment my spirit took over Eric's body in the hospital. Betty started to tear up. "So that is when my Eric crossed over?" I nodded yes and she wiped a tear from her eye. She cleared her throat. "So this whole time you have been pretending to be him, pretending to be my Eric? Did you not even consider that he had a family? A family that would be destroyed if they ever knew the truth?" Now it was my turn to start crying. "Betty, I am so sorry, I was so selfish. I didn't think about it until it was too late. All I could think about was getting back to Jess, whatever the consequences." Betty crossed her hands as if she was going to pray. "Does Jess know the truth?" I told her no but that I was going to tell her, she deserved to know too. Betty had a sad smile on her face. "You know, it's funny, you don't sound all that different than my Eric. He was a hopeless romantic just like you. I imagine he would probably have done the same thing as you given the chance, not that that makes it right. So, what happens now?"

I had to tell her the rest of what was happening, and I dreaded it more than anything. I took a deep breath. "Betty, there is something else I need to tell you and I just want you to know how sorry I am. The thing is what I have done violates God's laws and because of that since I have been here the Gates to Heaven have been closed. No one has been able to cross over fully while I remain in this body." I paused to let that sink in. It took a minute, but she finally connected the dots. She pulled her hands back from mine. "Do you mean...are you telling me that Eric has not crossed over?" My eyes went down to the table. I couldn't look at her when I answered, "Yes." It was all I could say. Nothing else would make this moment any easier for her. How do you prepare to hear that your only child is now a lost spirit floating somewhere in the ether? She got up and, deep in thought, paced around the room. I just sat there, not sure if I should say something. Eventually she came back over and sat down at the table with me. Betty cleared her throat. "So if what you are saying is true then this is happening all over the world and not just to Eric?" I took a deep breath. "Yes. Alistair says that until I return the Gates of Heaven will remain closed and the longer they remain closed the more souls will remain on Earth. He also said that at some point they will no longer be hidden from human eyes. And once that happens, that is pretty much it, the End of Days. I need to make things right." Betty took my hands. "Are you saying that I can see Eric? Have you seen him?" I shook my head no, but it was only a matter of time. "Betty, I am so sorry that I did this to you and your family. I am going to make things right whatever the consequences may be. If I have to go to Hell to let

Eric and everyone else in the world find peace, then that is what I have to do."

Betty looked at me with the eyes of a mother. She scooted her chair closer to me and put her hands on both of my cheeks. "Jack, God doesn't make mistakes. He is a just God, and an omniscient God. If you were allowed to do this, it is only because HE has allowed it to be. I feel that much like Job, this is a test. Man has free will and it is what we choose to do with that free will that determines what becomes of us when our time in this world is over. You may have been selfish, Jack, but realizing that selfishness and trying to fix the mistakes you have made is the right thing to do. And I believe that God forgives if you have light in your heart. I lost my son, Jack. Allow me to help you so that I may be able to say goodbye one final time." Hearing the kindness in her words was more than I could handle. I had selfishly taken away her sons everlasting happiness and yet here she was offering to help me. I began to sob uncontrollably. The guilt about what I had done came out in endless waves of tears. When I finally stopped crying enough to speak, I sat up and looked at Betty and wiped the tears out of my eyes. While she watched I took out my phone and made a call. When the call connected I said, "Jess, hi, it's Eric. Can you meet me in Central Park where we had our first date? I need to talk to you about something." She agreed and we hung up. Betty came over and wrapped her arms around me as more tears began to flow.

## 32

## BETTY

In life, we all try to prepare for the big moments that eventually come our way, whatever they may be. Whether it is the birth of a child, a new relationship, the death of a loved one, we try to prepare. But nothing could have prepared me for what just happened. When I heard the words "my name is not Eric" come out of Eric's mouth, I honestly don't know what I was first thinking. I just sat there blankly. What he said made no sense at all, I was looking at my son, my Eric, but there was something in the way he said it, the conviction in his voice. There was also a sense of exasperation, as if it was something he had been wanting to say for quite some time now. But how could that be true? And yet, even with my initial skepticism, I could feel the truth coming off of him in waves. Whether it was actually true was another matter entirely, but to him, this was the reality.

He continued and explained that he was actually a Guardian Angel named Jack. I should be mad; I should be furious. My son and his body have been violated by this interloper. And there was definitely a part of me that was

angry. My son wasn't my son. However, rather than being angry, I was, intrigued, I guess would be the best way to describe it. Was he telling the truth? And if so, I had so many questions, so many things I wanted to know. He explained how he had come to be in Eric's body. But where was my son? If the man I was looking at was no longer Eric, then where was Eric?

Bob's reaction was more one note. He was angry, angrier than I had seen him in a long while. But I wasn't about to let Bob stop Jack from telling me what was really happening. Bob isn't the only one with a temper. I don't like to be angry but when I am mad, I am heard, let's just put it that way. I sent Bob out for a walk so that Jack and I could speak.

As Bob was leaving, I was able to regain my composure.

And there was one feeling that had been lingering beneath all the others. It's hard to put into words what it was, but if I had to hazard a guess, I would call it warmth. The more I thought about it, the more I realized that what was happening was a validation of my faith. Guardian Angels are real, that must mean everything else was real. Angels are real. Heaven is real. God is real. What I was feeling, I can only imagine is similar to what we must feel when we cross over into Heaven. There was a peace that was slowly filling up my entire being. God must have heard all my prayers. I couldn't help but smile. Our Lord and Savior was truly up there listening. My faith now knows no bounds.

Perhaps that is why it was so easy for me to accept everything Jack was telling me.

I could tell Jack felt considerable remorse for what he had done. And I by no means approve of the lengths he has gone to, to come back to Earth. But I could understand why he had done it. If I were in his shoes and I had to see Bob suffering day in and day out, I can't say that I wouldn't have had the same desires, to find a way to come back to him. But on the flipside of that, he had taken possession of my son's body, my Eric. He was unable to cross over because of what Jack had done, rather than focus on that, I wanted to help Jack say goodbye to Jess. If that happens then everything would go back to the way it was and Eric could move on. I'll be sad if that happens but I could at least take comfort in the fact that Eric would be allowed into Heaven and he would be waiting there for Bob and me, when it was our time. I think it would have been easier to just be mad at Jack and God for allowing this to happen. But I think having true faith in God requires faith

in His plan. For God to have allowed this to happen, it must be for a reason. Whether or not we are to understand that reason or that purpose is not our place. And I truly believe that God is good. There are so many stories in the Bible where man is tested by God. Perhaps this is not Jack's test but my own.

A mother's love knows no bounds. We would do anything for our children. And maybe that is what my test is. Am I willing to allow the soul of my son to wander this plane in order for Jack to say goodbye to Jess?

For me, my choice is simple. I choose to help Jack say goodbye. I choose to have faith in man, faith in Jack that he will honor his words and his promise. I choose to believe in God and that Jack being God's creation is inherently good and just. Jack began to cry, and my heart went out to him. He was a good person, I could feel it in my bones, he had just gotten too wrapped up in his own desires and actions to truly consider the gravity of what he did. As I put my arms around him to comfort him his emotional floodgates opened. I held him tight. It reminded me of Eric as a child. He was always so proud and acted like he could handle everything. But no one is able to handle everything and when he would cry, it was all

consuming. Jack was very similar in that regard to Eric. Oddly, it brought a smile to my face. I may not have my Eric, but it made me think that if Jack and Eric had met when they were alive, they probably would have been friends, two peas in a pod. I told Jack I wanted to help him make things right and, in the hopes, that I was able to see my Eric one final time. And as he picked up the phone to make arrangements with Jess I prayed to God. I prayed for Jack and I prayed for myself. I prayed for the rest of humanity. But mostly, I prayed that God would grant me my wish, to have one final moment, however fleeting, with my Eric.

## 33

## JESS

I don't know if I was happy to hear from Eric or not because the call just felt so formal. He barely even said hello. All he wanted to do was to make plans to meet up. Of course, I agreed to meet him, I needed some answers from him, and I missed him, I'm not going to lie. Though we haven't known each other for that long the fact that I hadn't seen him in over a day just felt strange, it didn't feel right. I wanted to figure all of this out and move past it. My initial feelings were to just cut my losses and move on. But the more I thought about it, the more I realized I was ready to open up my heart again. And not to just anyone, to Eric. I'm ready for Eric to be my person. I can't believe I am even thinking that but I am glad that I am. I'm finally ready to open up my life to someone new and I want it to be Eric. He just needs to be honest about what happened in Paris.

Walking up to the fountain in Central Park my stomach was in knots. I just hoped everything went well, and we could figure this out together. As I turned the corner to head towards the fountain, I saw something I wasn't

expecting to see. Eric was there, waiting for me, but he was waiting there with his mother, Betty. Why would he bring his mother to talk to me? Did he tell her everything? I took a deep breath and walked over to them.

Betty gave me a big hug. It was nice to see her but if Eric and I are going to have a serious talk I can't do it in front of his mother. When our hug finished, she seemed to notice the confusion on my face. "Oh, don't worry, dear, I will leave you to it. I just came for moral support. E— He has something important to talk to you about." She leaned over and gave Eric a kiss. "It's time to do the right thing." I guess I have my answer; Eric is about to end things with me. But Jesus, I get that it is going to suck to hear that from Eric, but we are adults, did you really need to bring your mother here? It's not like someone died. Part of me just wanted to walk away, but I couldn't, I wanted to know why. I wanted to know why he doesn't want to give this a real shot. I wanted to know why he was such a coward. The more the questions flew around in my brain, the more pissed off I got!

Eric started to speak but I needed to get some things off my chest first. "You know what, Eric? If you weren't interested in me then why the hell did you sleep with me in Paris? Why the hell did you even agree to come with me on the trip in the first place?" He didn't say anything he just stared at me with this sadness in his eyes. Maybe I misjudged him and all this entirely. I just feel like a complete fool right now. I continued, "I wasn't asking for much, Eric, but you could have at least been honest with me and not just led me on. Did you do it just to go on a trip to Paris? I just don't understand how the trip started with some of the most amazing days in my entire life and then all of the sudden it falls apart and I don't even know why. And if you say it is because of the cemetery or whatever happened with that waiter I am going to punch you. I deserve to know the truth, Eric." I felt a little better getting all of that off my chest but only marginally. I'm just so confused and good or bad at least if I know the truth, I can process it.

He finally looked up at me. "Jess, it's not what you think at all. I'm sorry that I...I don't know. I'm sorry for so much. I don't even know where to begin." Well that wasn't what I was expecting. How am I supposed to take that? How many things has he done to hurt me? I was so confused. "What do you mean you're sorry for so much? Are you married?" He just laughed. "Eric, that is not a funny question, are you married?" He smiled at me. "No, I'm not married. I'm only laughing because that is a pretty ironic question, considering..." What the hell is he talking about? I continued, "Considering what? Eric, I need you to start explaining yourself!" He looked flustered "Jess, I'm trying but what I have to tell you isn't easy and I'm terrified about how you are going to react to what I have to say." I took his hands in mine, if I wanted to know what happened I needed to calm down too, attacking him isn't going to get either of us anywhere. I told him to just start talking, about anything and we can just take it from there.

He took a deep breath. "Jess, the first thing you need to know is that everything I felt, everything I feel is real. I don't want you to ever think my feelings for you are not genuine. And the fact that you even think that breaks my heart. You'll understand why when I get to the end of my story." Okay well it makes me feel a little better to know that what I was feeling was at least reciprocated. But if that is the case then what the hell happened and why is it ending? He continued, "The trip to Paris was perfect, for the most part anyway. I'd dreamed of going to Paris my entire life and to get to experience that with you was everything I could have hoped for and more.

Exploring the city with you, having dinner with you in the Eiffel Tower, walking home and in the rain together and making love all night. It was a fairy tale and I will cherish those memories for eternity." He got choked up, so I jumped in, "Then what happened, Eric?" He wiped a tear. "I'm getting to that. I guess you have some questions about the cemetery and what happened after." I nodded in agreement, and he continued, "Something happened. Something you didn't see... something you couldn't see and that is why I freaked out." What does that even mean, something I couldn't see? I took a step closer to him. "Eric, that doesn't make any sense. I don't understand what you are talking about. Did you know the man who died or his family?" He shook his head no. I could tell he was getting frustrated. "I am trying to figure out how to explain it to you, so you don't think I am a lunatic. It's not a simple explanation. It's complicated." Complicated. That is what people say when they have done something really messed up. Sorry, honey, did I forget to tell you that I have another family and we have seven kids together? But Eric isn't like those people. He is kind and sweet and, I thought, uncomplicated. But maybe I was wrong. I don't know what changed but maybe once he does tell me it won't be that big of a deal. At least I hope it won't. But I'm tired of him beating around the bush. I just need him to say it.

I pushed in closer to him. "Eric! Please ju—" He interrupted me, "Please don't call me Eric. My name isn't Eric." That sentence stopped me dead in my tracks. If his name isn't Eric, then what is it? I tried to ask him but the words didn't come. It was the last thing I thought he would say! My mind started reeling. I had so many questions going through my head. I took a step back. "So if your name isn't Eric, then what is it?" And then the questions just started pouring out of me. "Why would you lie to me about your name? Wait, I was your doctor, so I know your name is Eric! And your mom's name is Betty!" I looked back at Betty and she had a concerned look on her face. I turned back to Eric. "Wait, is that even your mom? Is this a scam? Are you some kind of con artist?" The more words came flying out of my mouth the more I began to question everything he had told me and everything I had felt since he woke up in the hospital. Am I just a fool?

Eric took a step towards me and I instinctively took another step back away from him. He pleaded with me, "Jess I can explain everything, I swear. I just don't know if you are going to like the answers you hear or if you are even going to believe them." I was over this. "We are so far past whether or not I believe what you are about to say. I deserve answers! I need answers NOW!" I was surprised at the anger in my voice. I could tell he was too because he looked shocked. But he wasn't looking at me he was looking behind me. I turned around to see what he was looking at but there was nothing there. At least I thought there was nothing there. All I could see was this grayish fog is the best way I can describe it, but that didn't make any sense because it was a bright sunny day. I turned back around to Eric (or whatever his name was) and I saw something I can't explain. The gray 'fog' was now behind him as well. What the hell was going on? It continued to thicken and had the consistency of the dense kind of fog you only see in places like San Francisco. Ever so slowly though, it began to take on a form, a shape, or several shapes for that matter. I squinted to try and get a better view of what was happening. It took a few more seconds but the gray swirling clouds took on a shape that was almost human. Eric could tell I was no longer paying attention to what he was saying. As he turned around the gray shapes finished materializing. They were people. Not solid. Not translucent, but something in between. My jaw hung open.

What was happening? What are they? I can't believe I am even about to say this but are they ghosts?

I felt like I was in a daze. Eric's words snapped me back to reality, "No! It's too soon. I'm not ready. I need more time!" What did he need more time for? He whipped around and started talking but I didn't hear a single word he said because of what I was staring at. Standing next to Eric was another gray shape in the form of someone I had recently becoming very familiar with. Standing next to Eric...was Eric.

## 34

## JACK

This is all going so wrong. Not that I expected it to go smoothly but I'd never seen her so upset. I didn't just want to blurt out what I needed to tell her, but I don't have a choice now. I was about to start talking when I saw the last thing I wanted to see appearing just over Jess's shoulders. Souls were beginning to appear and not just one but several. The misty gray swirling clouds I had become so familiar with in such a short time. Jess turned around and hesitated. I don't know if she saw what I was seeing but she definitely saw something.

She turned back around to me and the look on her face had changed. This time she was staring at something behind me. I turned around to see what she was looking at and my heart sank. More souls were beginning to appear behind me, and they weren't wispy shapes, these were quickly taking human form. It would only be a matter of moments until my secret was out. Mankind, and more importantly, Jess, was about to learn the truth.

The weather abruptly changed. The sunny sky darkened as thick clouds rolled in overhead. Lightning jumped from cloud to cloud and there was a steady rumble from the accompanying thunder. The winds began to whip around. It looked like the Heavens were about to open up, and maybe they were. Maybe this is how it all ends. In the Bible, the End of Days started with a bang. Maybe this was that bang? And what was next? I know in the Book of Revelations there were storms, but there were also plagues and famine and death. Was that next? Is this just the beginning?

Was this happening all over the world or was it just happening around me? Am I the epicenter? Three souls took full form directly in front of me; their sad eyes stared at me emptily. I reflexively yelled, "No! It's too soon. I'm not ready. I need more time!" I turned back around and started telling her the truth, the whole truth. But she wasn't listening to me. She looked completely in shock and she was staring at something just to my left. I looked over and my worst fear came true. Eric's soul was standing right next to me. The truth has come out before I could tell her. I didn't know what to say I just stood there in shock. Jess looked just as shocked and terrified at the same time, both of us at a complete loss for words. I took a step towards her and she took several away from me. This was all spiraling out of control, and I didn't know what to do. We

were both snapped out of our respective dazes by Betty screaming when she saw her son, her real son standing next to me. Jess shook her head like she was shaking off the cobwebs and looked at me. "I don't know what the fuck is going on, but I can't do this." She turned and ran away from me at the same time that Betty was running towards me, well not me but Eric. As she got closer, she yelled, "Go after her!" I wanted to be there to help her with her son because she had been so accepting of what I had done but I listened to her and I took off running after Jess. The thunder continued to rumble and gain in intensity as I chased after her. As I ran through the park, the wind blew leaves and trees all around. Next, bolts of lightning began to crash down around the park. They were getting closer and closer, no longer skipping between the clouds. The storm was getting worse by the minute. How long would it be before someone was injured? Or killed? As these thoughts swirled in my head, a torrential downpour began. Joggers scattered for shelter. Things were quickly spiraling out of control.

I was also seeing more and more spirits whizzing by me as I ran. I came around a bend and I saw Jess and did my best to pick up speed to catch her. She was too fast though and I was only able to gain on her a little bit. I screamed, "JESS, PLEASE STOP!" She continued to run. "SCREW YOU, ERIC!" With my options running out I did the one thing I had said I didn't want to do with Jess. I blurted out the truth, "JESS, I'M JACK!" It took only a second for the words to reach her and she stopped dead in her tracks. Her hair had been matted down from the heavy rain. She seemed completely oblivious to the chaos around her. She turned around and the anger in her face was something I had never seen on her before. I mean sure she had been mad at me often when I was alive, but this was more than just mad.

She started walking towards me, her pace quickening with each step. She was upon me before I even realized what she was planning to do. Her hand connected with my cheek so hard that it made my ears ring. I stumbled to the right before I managed to catch by balance. When I looked at her there was pure venom in her eyes. Before she turned and walked away from me, she leaned in and through gritted teeth said, "How dare you, Eric! I hope you burn in hell for this!" How is that for irony, right?

My eyes were stinging from the smack, but I didn't have a choice anymore I couldn't let her walk away. I shook off the pain and followed her. "Jess, please stop! Please,

I am telling you the truth." She didn't say a word she just kept walking. How am I supposed to convince her that I am me, that I am Jack? I don't look like me and there is no way for her to see me. I needed to make things right with her before I wasn't able to anymore. Everything is happening fast now and any minute I might be gone. And then it came to me. Only someone who really knew Jess would know her favorite quote, our favorite quote from Oscar Wilde. It was worth a shot. I closed my eyes and went for it. "You don't love someone for their looks, or their clothes, or their fancy car..." She stopped and turned around and finished the rest of the quote with me at the same time that I did, "... but because they sing a song that only you can hear." She was in shock but intrigued. It was written all over her face. She took a few steps towards me. "How do you know that?" I cautiously took a step towards her. "Because I am telling the truth. J, it is me. I'm Jack." She shook her head. "That isn't possible. This is some kind of trick. Why are you doing this, Eric?" I hadn't gotten through to her, she still thought this was some kind of awful trick I was playing on her. I continued, "Jess, please let me explain. I did die. I did leave you and I went to Heaven, but I came back, I came back for you." She

didn't believe me. "What do you mean you came back? Is that even possible? And if this is true, why do you look like someone else? Why don't you look like Jack?" All I can do is tell her the absolute truth and hope for the best. I started from the beginning, "Jess, when I died I went to Heaven and I found out that we are soulmates. I already knew that, but you see, the thing I came to find out about soulmates is that if for some reason one is taken from the other, they have the choice to become a Guardian Angel. So that is what I did. I came back to you, only you couldn't see me, couldn't see that I was there. I couldn't touch you or console you. I watched you, trapped in your own sadness, unable to move on from what happened to me. I sat with you every night as you watched our engagement video and cried. But I couldn't do it any longer. I couldn't just sit by and watch you not living your life. I needed to find a way to come back to you to show you that it is okay to move on, that it is okay to say goodbye to me, so I found a loophole."

By this point Jess was in tears. "How am I supposed to believe any of this? Everyone knew I was just hiding in my apartment that isn't news. I don't believe you. The Jack I knew wouldn't do something like this. This is just cruel."

I continued, "I promise you that this is the truth, I don't know how to convince you that I am your Jack." I was losing her. She was becoming more and more angry. "Stop lying, Eric! Why are you doing this to me? What did I do to deserve this? I have been nothing but nice to you. I was falling for you. How can you be this heartless?" I needed something that would cut through everything and get to her, but I didn't know what that was. And then it hit me like a ton of bricks. She revealed something at my funeral that no one knew. I walked up to her and took her by the arms. She tried to pull away, but I wouldn't let her. I looked into her eyes. "The first time we met wasn't in high school like I thought. I heard the truth at my funeral. You were the girl with the lemonade stand. I never knew that. Why did you never tell me the truth?" Her eyebrows raised slightly and her lips parted. I've gotten through to her. She looked in shock. "But how...I...I...is it really you, Jack?" I moved my hands up to her cheeks and looked deeply into her eyes and thought to myself please just see me in Eric's eyes, see through them, see me. I brushed a wet strand of hair away from her face. "it's me, J, I promise." She reacted to me calling her J. I only ever called her that when we were alone, she had to know now that it was me. And then I leaned in and kissed her, and she let me. And just for a moment everything was perfect. She kissed me back and I slid my hands around her waist and I just wanted to stay in this moment for eternity. But the moment passed. She pulled back and touched her left hand to her lips. Her right hand stayed in mine and I unconsciously traced an infinity symbol with my thumb on the inside of her palm, like I used to do when I was alive. Her eyes widened and she looked down at her hand. I could almost see the lightbulb go on above her head. "It is you! Jack...you used to that when we held hands." Her walls crumbled and she threw her arms around me in tears. I held her as tightly as I could. I wanted to hold her as long as I was able. I didn't know how much time I had left. She pulled back and wiped tears from her eyes. "How is this even possible?" She was interrupted by a bolt of lightning splitting a tree in half less than a hundred yards from where we were standing. We should get out of the storm, but neither of us wanted to move.

Now that I had gotten through to her I needed her to know everything. I sighed deeply. "Jess, there is something I need to tell you. Something that, honestly, I don't know how you are going to take, but I did it for you. I did all of this for you. That day back in the hospital Eric did pass away and I possessed his body." She took a step back. "What do you mean 'possessed'?" I continued, "I put my soul into his body the moment he passed. That was when he flat-lined and before I connected with his body. It was the only way I could come back to you, the only way you would be able to physically see me and touch me." Her eyebrows furrowed. "So you did all this to just touch me again?

Jack, you have been lying to everyone this entire time. I mean, Eric's family...how could you do something like that?" She was right, I had thought this was going to be some grand gesture, but I had stolen something, the most precious thing, and I had been living a lie for weeks now. I needed to make it right. "Betty knows the truth, Jess. I told her before I came here. That is why she's here, she wanted to help me say goodbye to you." She took another step back. "What do you mean 'goodbye'? Where are you going?"

It was the moment of truth. "Jess, there is more. When I did what I did there were consequences." She looked me in the eyes and I cleared my throat. "What I did, crossing back over to this plane, well, it's a violation of the rules of Heaven, of God's law and because of that the Gates of Heaven are closed. No one is able to cross over because of what I have done, and no one will be able to cross over until I go back. Only I don't think Heaven is where I am heading." I could see that my words crushed her. Honestly, how did I expect her to take the news? She looked around at the storm and the now-visible souls. "So you mean that those, I don't even know what word to use, those gray swirls, those 'people', those are the souls of people who have died and can't cross over? Wait, so what the waiter in France saw was real?" I nodded yes. She continued, "And this is all happening because of me?" She pulled back from me reeling. "How could you do this? The Jack I knew, the man I loved would not be capable of something so horrible. How could you do it? My God, all those people, trapped here..." Her words faded under the gravity of what I had done to her. I wanted to tell her it was only meant to be temporary, that I just wanted to show her how to live her life again, but I knew it was going to fall on deaf ears.

All she could see was the damage I had done to the world because of her. She continued taking steps away from me and then turned and ran without saying a word. I wanted to chase after her, but I needed to give her time. I just hoped I had enough time to say goodbye. I stood there at the heart of the storm, hopeless and alone.

# 35

# JESS

My world is spinning. How is this happening? Is it even true? I don't know what to believe. On the one hand a lot of what he knows about me he could have easily found out. But on the other hand, there are some things he just couldn't know. And I know this sounds crazy, but my gut tells me that what he is saying is the truth. I don't even know what he had to go through to come back to me but the consequences of what he has done are more than I can handle. How am I supposed to be okay with this? I can't be that selfish. Of course, I want him to stay with me. Now that I know it is him there is so much I want to do, so many things I want to say but I don't know how to say any of them. My Jack would have never done what he did, but then again, he DID do it so maybe I didn't know Jack as well as I thought. Maybe I shouldn't have run away from him, maybe I should have stayed and listened to everything he had to say but I just couldn't. Finding out that you are partially responsible for what could be the end of the world is just a lot to process. How am I supposed to just

sit by knowing that so many people, alive and dead, are suffering because of what he did? Even though it wasn't me who did this, now that I know the truth I am just as complicit as he is if he chooses to do nothing.

But how could he possibly do nothing? The man I loved wouldn't just sit idly by while people suffered. If we are indeed soulmates, and I do believe we are, he would know that I couldn't live with myself if that happened. As I sat in the taxi driving through the city, all I could think about were those poor souls and their poor families, especially Eric, Betty, and Bob. Seeing Eric's soul standing next to his body was by far the most surreal moment of my life. He just looked so sad and confused, like someone who was sleepwalking. He was there but he wasn't there. I wondered what if anything he was thinking or feeling. I mean whether you believe in Heaven or not you hope that you just go somewhere safe or maybe you think that you move on to the next plane of existence. But whatever it is that you believe what had happened to Eric was cruel. Everything was taken away from him and now he was trapped. And poor Betty, how did she handle everything when Jack told her the truth? She is a saint. How did she manage to forgive Jack for what he had done to her son? And how heartbreaking it must have been for her to see the soul of her only son just trapped like that.

I don't even know what to do now. I am feeling so many emotions that I am just overwhelmed. The weather outside was continuing to get worse. The heavy rain had now turned into hail. Little pellets of ice were rhythmically tapping on the roof as we drove. Was this storm because of Jack? I was looking out the window in a daze when we passed a church. I yelled to the taxi driver to pull over. Given the circumstances it was the only thing that made sense. I needed to talk to someone who knew more about this than I did. Who better to talk to than a priest right? Getting out of the taxi, I saw more souls appearing, in the street. I can't help but feel that things are escalating, and we are running out of time. More and more people were noticing that something was happening around them, something they couldn't explain. You could almost taste the fear in the air. Walking into the church my head was spinning.

The inside of the church was beautiful and massive. The interior rose a hundred feet into the air. The sides were lined with stained glass windows with individual panels highlighting various passages from the Bible.

Several parishioners were sitting scattered in the pews deep in prayer. I figured it would be more crowded considering what was going on outside, but maybe the gravity of what was happening hadn't reached a fever pitch just yet. It was only a matter of time before it did, and then what would everyone do?

I walked forward towards the altar. Off to the left were several confessional boxes. I figured that was as good a place to go as any. I opened the door and closed it behind me. I took a seat on the bench and instantly felt claustrophobic. I sat there for a few moments in silence trying to gather my thoughts. I mean how do you tell a priest that your dead ex-fiancé has come back to life and currently, is inhabiting the body of someone else. It's not like that kind of information just rolls off the tongue. I heard the other door open and the priest enter. It took a moment but then the small door opened leaving just the screen between us. It had been so long since I had been to confession, I almost forgot how it starts so I sat there briefly in silence. But then I remember I need to start it off with, "Bless me, Father, for I have sinned. It has been longer than I can remember since my last confession." The priest introduced himself as Father Xavier. "And what brings you here today, my child?" I didn't really know how

to start other than to just jump right in. "Father Xavier, have you noticed anything out of the ordinary the last few days? Have you heard any stories from other parishioners about seeing strange things around the city?" Father Xavier said he had not. "What exactly are you asking?" I figured I would try another route. "So I know you believe in Heaven, obviously—" He interrupted, "And, do you? Believe in Heaven, that is?" I paused for a moment. "I guess so, to be honest I've never really given it that much thought. Well I'm pretty sure after the day I have had that Heaven is real, which sort of makes me think the other place is real too." I was getting off topic. "Anyway, are there like laws in Heaven, like laws for Angels or something?" Ugh, could I sound less intelligent right now? Father Xavier took a few deep breaths. "Yes of course there are Heavenly laws. Some people refer to them as Divine Laws. They are put in place by God much like the laws we have here on Earth. The first of the Divine Laws has to do with Obedience." Now it was my turn to interrupt. "Well, what happens if say someone were to disobey those laws, I mean not someone obviously, like what would happen if, for example, an Angel or hypothetically, a Guardian Angel, disobeyed Divine Law?" This time he didn't hesitate. "Well Lucifer disobeyed the

word of God and I assume you know how that turned out for him. He turned his back on Heaven and he was cast out. Why do you ask these questions, I'm sorry, what was your name?" I told him my name and he continued, "Why are you so concerned with Divine Law, Jess?" Well what I wanted to tell him was to just wait around for a little while, eventually when he saw souls appearing he would understand what I was talking about. But I didn't have that kind of time. And all I kept thinking was is Jack going to go to Hell for what he has done? I have to believe that if there is a Heaven then there is a Hell. Oh God! Is that why Jack was trying to make things right now? Is that one of the consequences that he was talking about? There has to be something I can do to help him, even if that means saying goodbye forever.

I needed to get to the point. "Father, say a Guardian Angel did disobey Divine Law, is there a way to fix things? Can they seek penance or something like that?" Father Xavier started to speak but then hesitated. "Jess, it might be easier if we didn't speak in metaphors but if that makes you more comfortable than so be it. The God that I believe in is and a forgiving God so if an 'Angel'"—I could almost hear him doing air quotes when he said Angel—"violates

Divine Law he can indeed seek penance for God knows what is in our hearts. Jess, the Lord works in mysterious ways so perhaps whatever has happened is all part of God's plan." I thought to myself, I really doubt that. And this isn't helping me at all, it is just making me more confused. I just need to get out of here and go and find Jack. However, this ended it needed to end and it needed to end now. I thanked Father Xavier for speaking with me and he tried to continue but I had already opened the door and was halfway down the aisle to the exit when I heard the confessional box open behind me. I didn't turn back around until I got to the door. I glanced back and Father Xavier was staring at several souls that had appeared just near the confessional box. If his jaw could hit the floor I think it would have. He then looked over in my direction and in that moment, he understood that what I had been talking about wasn't a metaphor at all. He called to me but I had no time to console him so I walked out the door into the storm. In the few minutes that I had been inside, everything had gotten much worse. Things were spiraling quickly.

I was hoping that speaking to Father Xavier would help me figure out what to do, but it didn't. How was I going to help Jack make this right? How do you apologize to God?

Would he even listen? I can't believe that I am even thinking these questions but whether I believed it or not yesterday, today I have no choice but to believe that it is true. Heaven. Hell. Angels. That is a lot to process to be forced to accept that all those abstract ideas aren't abstract at all. I needed to figure out what my next move was. I needed to find Jack. I got to the intersection and pressed the button for the crosswalk. I could barely see in front of me, the rain was coming down so hard now. I pulled my jacket up over my head to give myself a little more protection. I took out my phone and dialed Eric, Jack. The light turned and the white figure lit up to signal that it was safe to cross the street. I stepped out into the intersection as the phone starting to ring.

## JESS

I was so consumed with getting a hold of Jack that I didn't even hear him scream my name from across the street, or see the car barreling towards me...

# 36

## JACK

Everything was falling apart. The storm outside continued to worsen. The rain was now coming down sideways. Each successive drop felt like a tiny needle stinging me all over my body. Everywhere I turned, people were in a panic. The world was hurtling towards its conclusion. I left the park and passed an electronics store with a half dozen TVs on display in the window. Each monitor was playing the news from a different part of the world. Though they were showing different cities around the globe, the scenes were the same, everything was chaos. Earthquakes in Japan. Floods in India. Riots in Sao Paolo. It was all ending because of what I had done. I needed to find Jess. I was out of time, but I didn't know where to start. I went by the hospital but no one had seen her since before she went to Paris. I tried calling her a few times but she wasn't answering the phone. The streets were jammed with people trying to get out of the city. I didn't have time to wait for a taxi so I ran from the hospital to her apartment. Along the way, more and more souls continued to appear, causing the fear and paranoia to grow

   exponentially. Fear is contagious. The first domino had fallen. How long before the last domino fell? I just hoped I had enough time to find Jess to say goodbye. I still hadn't even figured out how to make things right. I started having a sinking feeling in my gut. What if I ran out of time? What if I never got to say goodbye to Jess? How would she deal with our conversation in the park being the last time that she ever spoke to me? I wonder if in time she could convince herself than none of it was real. I was beginning to feel more and more hopeless like all of this was for nothing. But I pressed on, I had to, until I wasn't able to anymore. I got to her building and waved to the doorman as I ran inside, not even giving him a chance to stop me. I was in the elevator with the doors closing before he even made it close enough to attempt to stop me.

I got to Jess's door and pounded but there was no answer. Where was she? I was running out of options. I had one final idea. It was the last thing I wanted to do but I felt like I didn't have a choice. I called out for Alistair but he didn't come. Had he turned his back on me too? The despair continued to grow in my heart. I felt lost. I felt hopeless. I turned to head back to the elevator and frantically pressed the button, every second counted at

this point. As the doors opened I saw Alistair inside carrying a folder, and my body was flooded with relief. He would be able to help me figure this out. At least I hoped so. But the look on his face said the opposite. I had never seen him look so sad and sullen before. He stepped off the elevator. Everything about him seemed muted, even the red on his coat seemed to have faded several shades since the last time I saw him. I tried to calm my nerves as he approached. "Alistair, I need your help. I told Jess the truth and now I can't find her. Can you help me find her, please? I need to say goodbye. I need to make this right.

I'm ready to go back." His head sank further towards the ground. He couldn't even look me in the eye. He said softly, "It's too late." My heart sank.

How can it be too late? Is he here to take me back? Or is he here to take me somewhere else? I tried my best to steady my breathing. "Alistair, what do you mean 'it's too late?'" He looked up at me and there was a curious mixture of anger and sadness in his eyes. He handed me the folder. "I told you not to do this, but did you listen? No! I told you there would be consequences but did you heed my warning? No!" My eyes widened. "Alistair, what is about to happen?" He gestured to the folder that was now in my hand.

I slowly opened it as he talked. "Sometimes the greatest punishment is not what happens to oneself, but rather the pain and regret of living with what has happened to others."

I didn't have time for Alistair's fortune cookie responses but the second I opened the folder it all made sense. I was holding Jess's folder from the Office of Human Resources and what I saw written on the paper shattered my heart into a million pieces. I was looking at the date of Jess's death and that date had been changed to today. I fell to my knees. With tears streaming down my face I pleaded with Alistair, "I'll come back, just please don't do this. It's not too late to fix things. It's not too late to make this right!" He kneeled down near me. "I'm afraid that it is too late. Her course has been altered. You will remain on this plane for eternity without her. Once her soul crosses over, the debt, your debt, will have been paid. The balance will be restored and the Gates will re-open. I am sorry, Jack." I got to my feet. "No! Please, this can't be how it ends, she is innocent. Take me instead, take me to Heaven to face punishment or take me to Hell I don't care but just please don't do this to her." The sadness in his eyes returned. "Hell means different things to us all. Your hell is a life without Jess, an eternal life without Jess. A life for a life. You will never again see her smile, hear her voice. You are doomed to walk the streets alone until the end of days."

No! Jess doesn't deserve this. She deserves so much more than this. She deserves to have a family, to grow old, to live! My sadness was replaced by anger. How could God be so cruel? I did this. I should be punished. Jess was an innocent victim in all this. I am the villain. I looked at the fine print on the paper. She dies in a car accident. I can stop this. I can make this right. I grabbed Alistair by the lapels of his coat and slammed him up against the wall. "WHERE DOES IT HAPPEN? TELL ME NOW!" He flicked me away like I was a bug on his windshield. How was he able to touch me now? I didn't have time to figure that out. I slammed into the wall, it knocked the wind out of me and I slid down to the floor. I looked up at him pleadingly. "Alistair, help me. Let me make this right." He closed his eyes. "St. Anthony's Church, hurry." That church is only a few blocks from her apartment. I can make it! I have to!

I didn't wait another moment. I got up and ran for the stairwell, not having time to wait for the elevator. I ran down the stairs as fast as I could and back out the front

door of the building, into the storm. I made a left and ran as fast as my legs would take me. I didn't care what happened to me, all I cared about was making it to Jess in time. I crossed the first block with ease. The next block was more congested but I pushed my way through the crowd.

As soon as the church came into view my phone started to ring. I tried to pull it out to see who was calling me and it was Jess! I was going to answer but there was no need to, I saw her on the other side of the street, about to walk into the crosswalk. I screamed for her but she didn't hear me. My lungs burned but I ran faster, I had to get to her. As I ran into the crosswalk, I heard a loud screech coming from up the block. A large black Escalade was barreling towards Jess. I didn't stop running. "JESS! LOOK OUT!" She looked up at me. "JACK!" She didn't see the car at all. I felt like I was about to collapse from exhaustion but I had to get to her. I willed myself to move faster, but with every step I took the Escalade moved ten feet closer to her. I screamed again for her to look out. This time she heard me. She turned her head to the left. The Escalade was mere feet from her. I leaped towards her.

Please, God, I know you're pissed at me right now, but please don't do this, please let me get there in time...

# 37

## JESS

I didn't think that this was how my life was going to end. I closed my eyes waiting for the impact of the car but I felt another impact. I opened them just in time to see Jack pushing me out of the way. I slammed backwards onto the sidewalk barely missing the Escalade. Jack wasn't so lucky. The Escalade hit him full force sending him flying a hundred yards up the street. He landed in a crumpled heap. I screamed and ran to him not even seeing that the Escalade had veered off to the left into oncoming traffic.

When I got to him there was blood everywhere. It made me think of what Jack looked like in the bodega all those years ago. I tried to wake him up but there was no use he was gone. Tears streamed down my face. The world faded away. I picked him up to hold him. He was still warm. My tears mixed with the blood on his face and made light pink streaks. I looked up. The last thing I saw was a pair of headlights inches from my face. I closed my eyes and waited for the impact...

# 38

## JACK & JESS

I waited for the impact but it never came. When I opened my eyes, I was no longer on the street outside the church. I wasn't sure where I was. I wasn't sure what happened. Did a car just hit me? Am I dead? I looked around to try and figure out where I was but there were no surroundings to look at. I was surrounded by nothing. It was as if I were in a giant white room that was so large you couldn't see any of the walls because they were so far off in the distance. I should be terrified but I wasn't.

There was something peaceful about this place, wherever I was. Maybe this was the white light people saw when they passed over. If it was I guess I know what happened to me but if I am gone it didn't seem to bother me all that much. Maybe that is the other thing that happens when you die; the things that happened to you in life fade away. But what am I supposed to do now? Is this Heaven? I called out to see if anyone could hear me. "Hello! Is anyone there? Am I in Heaven?" I heard a response from behind me. It was a simple, "No," but it wasn't the word that stopped me in my tracks. It was the voice. It was a voice I thought I would

never hear again. I closed my eyes, could it be true? I turned around and slowly opened my eyes and sure enough it is who I hoped it would be. And he was just as handsome as I remember with his smile that turned down slightly at the end. It was Jack. Without even thinking I just ran to him and threw my arms around him. We must both be dead, but in this moment, I don't care, all I cared about was that a moment I thought would never happen again is happening and I didn't want it to end. I wanted to stay in this embrace for eternity, that, would be Heaven, to me. I pulled back from him and looked him in the eyes. I missed those eyes staring back at me.

* * *

The last thing I remember was running across the street to push Jess out of the way of the Escalade that was about to hit her. Maybe I didn't get there in time? Maybe I did but instead of saving her we both died together? It didn't matter. It was over. But why are we together? I don't know what is going to happen but I will be forever grateful for this moment. Jess can see me, the real me, and she can touch me. I can hold her. I can kiss her. I could tell that she had questions. I know when I died the first time I had so many questions. She looked at me and smiled.

"So it was all true? Everything you were telling me?" I nodded yes. She continued, "But what happens now?" I asked her what the last thing she remembered was. She looked away briefly. "I was crossing the street and I didn't see the car coming but I did see Eric, I mean you, I can't believe this is all happening. But I saw you and just before the car hit me you managed to push me out of the way but the car hit you. I ran over to you to see if you were alive but you weren't. The last thing I remember is seeing a pair of headlights coming towards me." It would have broken my heart if I still had one but all I felt was the ache I've had in my chest since before all of this started. I took her hands in mine. "Jess, I am so sorry. This wasn't supposed to happen to you. Your life was cut short because of me. If I could go back and change things I would."

* * *

I was so excited to see Jack that I had almost forgotten about everything that was happening. "What happened to Eric? Where is he? Do you think he crossed over when we died? Do you think everyone is able to cross over now?" It turns out I had way more questions than I realized. Jack sighed. "I don't know, Jess. All I can hope is that Eric is at peace now. I hope everything is back to normal and the Gates of Heaven are now open and everything is as it should be." From behind me I heard a voice I didn't recognize say, "Well, not entirely." I turned around to see two men, one was a tall man dressed in a red coat.

He looked like he was straight out of some old movie set in Victorian England. But I did recognize the man standing next to him. It was Eric. He didn't say a word but he did have a peaceful smile on his face.

* * *

I was so glad to see Alistair. It meant I wasn't in hell so maybe there was still hope for me but it also meant that hopefully we would get some answers. It was hard to see Eric after what I had done to him but I am glad that he can now be at peace. I took Jess by the hand and we walked over to them. "It's nice to see you, Alistair. Eric, I hope you can forgive me. I don't know if there will ever be a way for me to make things right but know that I will be eternally sorry for everything that has happened." He didn't say a word and his expression didn't change. It was almost a smile but not quiet. There was an element of curiosity to his expression, much like a small child seeing something for the first time. Maybe he just hadn't adjusted to the fact that he had crossed over. I know it took me a

little while to fully comprehend what had happened to me. I turned to Alistair. "So what happens now?" Alistair took a step towards me. "It seems your situation has changed." Cryptic as always, Alistair. I raised my eyebrows. "And what does that mean? Does that mean I'm not going to—" Alistair cut me off, "It means that this was a test. Humans make mistakes. You are not perfect creatures, Jack. You have the gift of free will but it is what you choose to do with that choice that makes all the difference." What part of this was a test? All of it? I didn't understand and neither did Jess because she looked more confused than I did. I turned back to Alistair and Eric. "So this was ALL a test? You knew that I would find a way to come back to Jess?" He shook is his head no. "No one, well almost no one, could have predicted that you would find a way back to Earth. The test was to see what you would do when you found out that Jess's life had been altered. What would you be willing to do, what would you be willing to sacrifice for her?" Without hesitation I said, "I would sacrifice everything for her, it's always been about her." Alistair smiled. "Exactly, you were willing to risk eternal damnation to save her life. Not everyone in your shoes would have made the same choice."

Alistair stepped back next to Eric, who finally spoke. "Do you know the story of Adam and Eve?" I was confused as to what that had to do with anything but we both nodded yes. He continued, "Humans often miss the point of that story. Eve made a bad decision and had to leave the Garden of Eden but the choice in the story is Adam's. He could have easily chosen to say goodbye to Eve and remained in the Garden but he chose to leave with her. It is always about choice. And, Jack, the choice you made to save Jess regardless of the consequences for yourself was a selfless choice." Eric sounded like Alistair. For the first time, I felt a sense of hope, maybe this all wouldn't end how I had thought. Alistair smiled, but I had so many questions. At this, Eric smiled fully and I was filled with warmth that ran through my whole body. It was a feeling that was indescribable. It made me feel like home.

* * *

I gripped Jack's hand tighter. I looked over at Eric and he smiled, and I smiled back. The love that radiated from him was something I can't put into words, I just knew that everything was going to be all right. I could feel it in every inch of my body as if I were standing in the sun and being warmed from the inside out.

* * *

My whole being tingled and I looked at Alistair and understood why. My eyes widened and he nodded in confirmation. I squeezed Jess's hand and we looked deep into each other's eyes. Then I looked over at Eric and I wasn't sure if I should say anything but I figured when would I ever have this opportunity again. "Are you God?" Eric walked towards us and put one hand on each of our cheeks. In an instant, I had my answer...

# 39

# EPILOGUE

It had been a long night in the maternity ward. There must have been something in the air because the nursery was packed with well over twenty newborns. Mary was going on hour fifteen of her shift. Though she loved her job days like today really took it out of her. She was in her mid-thirties, but currently felt twice her age. There were so many babies born today that the normally spacious nursery was filled beyond capacity. Usually she would make sure there was enough space between all of the bassinets but not tonight, they were all lined up with each bassinet touching the one next to it. She was getting too old for days like today. The door to the nursery opened and Elsie, another nurse walked in. Elsie was the oldest nurse at the hospital and she was everyone's surrogate mom. She made her way over to Mary. "How are things going in here?" Mary tried to smile but she was too tired. "I think I just need a nap, it's been one of those days." Elsie smiled. "Don't I know it, I just tucked in my last, Mama, so I think we are done for the night." Mary laughed. "Thank God!" She jokingly put her head on Elsie's shoulder and Elsie responded in kind by putting her arm around Mary's and rubbing gently. Mary

closed her eyes. She was so tired she could almost fall asleep like this.

Elsie giggled. "Would you look at that!" Mary opened her eyes and a big smile came across her face. It wasn't something you see every day. While all the babies around them cried in the center of the nursery, a newborn baby girl had reached up and was holding hands with the little boy in the next bassinet.

## THE END

CPSIA information can be obtained
at www.ICGtesting.com
Printed in the USA
LVHW041622261121
704543LV00010B/145